Now that he was living every other week at different houses, Tree always forgot to pack something.

His warm gloves were at his mother's house.

His good sneakers were, too. He needed them for basketball practice, but it would take a lot more than sneakers to make him good at the game.

He couldn't remember if he packed underwear.

Probably not.

A strong, cold wind whipped through the park. He'd been playing here, walking here for so many years. But since his parents got divorced, it felt like a different place.

Up the stairs to the north was where he'd go when he was staying at his mom's new house.

Across the footbridge to the south was where his dad and grandfather lived.

So much had changed since the summer.

He started walking toward his father's house, past a lone Salvation Army trumpeter playing Christmas carols. Fished in his pocket, found a dollar, put it in the red bucket.

Mrs. Stench's dog, Fang, trotted toward him, barking mean.

"Fang, be nice." Mrs. Stench yanked on the expanding leash, lurched forward.

Fang ran up to the white oak, lifted his leg, and peed on the noble gray bark.

Tree sighed deep; cold air came out.

Being a tree isn't easy.

Books by

JOAN BAUER

STAND TALL

JOAN BAUER

STAND TALL

speak
An Imprint of Penguin Group (USA) Inc.

SPEAK
Published by the Penguin Group
Penguin Group (USA) Inc., 345 Hudson Street, New York, New York 10014, U.S.A.
Penguin Group (Canada), 10 Alcorn Avenue, Toronto, Ontario, Canada M4V 3B2
(a division of Pearson Penguin Canada Inc.)
Penguin Books Ltd, 80 Strand, London WC2R 0RL, England
Penguin Ireland, 25 St Stephen's Green, Dublin 2, Ireland (a division of Penguin Books Ltd)
Penguin Group (Australia), 250 Camberwell Road, Camberwell, Victoria 3124, Australia
(a division of Pearson Australia Group Pty Ltd)
Penguin Books India Pvt Ltd, 11 Community Centre,
Panchsheel Park, New Delhi - 110 017, India
Penguin Group (NZ), Cnr Airborne and Rosedale Roads, Albany,
Auckland 1310, New Zealand (a division of Pearson New Zealand Ltd)
Penguin Books (South Africa) (Pty) Ltd, 24 Sturdee Avenue,
Rosebank, Johannesburg 2196, South Africa

Registered Offices: Penguin Books Ltd, 80 Strand, London WC2R 0RL, England

First published in the United States of America by G. P. Putnam's Sons,
a division of Penguin Putnam Books for Young Readers, 2002
Published by Speak, an imprint of Penguin Group (USA) Inc., 2004
This edition published by Speak, an imprint of Penguin Group (USA) Inc., 2005

10

Copyright © Joan Bauer, 2002
All rights reserved

THE LIBRARY OF CONGRESS HAS CATALOGED THE G. P. PUTNAM'S SONS EDITION AS FOLLOWS:
Bauer, Joan. Stand tall / Joan Bauer.
p. cm.
Summary: Tree, a six-foot-three-inch twelve-year-old, copes with his parents'
recent divorce and his failure as an athlete by helping his grandfather,
a Vietnam vet and recent amputee, and Sophie, a new girl at school.
ISBN: 0-399-23473-X (hc)
[1. Divorce—Fiction. 2. Grandfathers—Fiction. 3. Size—Fiction.
4. Individuality—Fiction. 5. Schools—Fiction.] I. Title.
PZ7.B32615Sr 2002 [Fic]—dc21 2002023876

Speak ISBN 0-14-240427-6

Printed in the United States of America

FOR EVAN, MY HERO

ACKNOWLEDGMENTS ■ Abundant thanks to: Nancy Paulsen, my editor, for her wisdom, grace, and deft handling of this story. George Nicholson, my agent, who read every draft and offered superb counsel during the writing of this book. Jean Bauer, my daughter, who told me I could and would finish this book, despite evidence to the contrary. Marjorie Good, my mother, who has given me a lifetime of inspiration. Pastor JoAnn Clark, Laura Smalley, and Rita Zuidema, who stand firm during the writing of all my stories.

Thanks to all who shared the realities and struggles of Vietnam vets, amputees, and the extremely tall: Colonel Jeffrey Thompson, M.D., United States Air Force, who provided not just medical facts, but profound thoughts on the realities of war. Twala Maresh, Clinical Instructor II, M.S.P.T., University of Central Arkansas—who taught me the day-to-day struggles, victories, and mechanics of working with amputees. Eileen R. Ascher, L.O.T., Coordinator of Rehabilitation Services at The Rehabilitation Center of Southwestern Connecticut, Inc., who showed me the power of rehab at work, and along with physical therapist Laurie Schacht, answered endless questions *and* introduced me to John DeMaio, a retired fireman and recent amputee. John's courage and heart inspired many characters in this novel. Don Shirley, a veteran and children's writer, who forwarded me useful information about VA Hospitals and Vietnam. Vicki Walker at Tall Persons Club of Great Britain and Ireland—her insights as a mother of tall children helped greatly, as did the Tall Persons Club organization. Alex Tarshis, who shared his experiences in the wild world of height.

To every thing there is a season,
And a time to every purpose under heaven:
A time to be born and a time to die,
A time to plant and a time to uproot,
A time to kill and a time to heal,
A time to tear down and a time to build,
A time to weep and a time to laugh,
A time to mourn and a time to dance,
A time to scatter stones and a time to gather them,
A time to embrace and a time to refrain,
A time to search and a time to give up,
A time to keep and a time to throw away,
A time to tear and a time to mend,
A time to be silent and a time to speak,
A time to love and a time to hate,
A time for war and a time for peace.

—ECCLESIASTES 3:1–8

CHAPTER ONE

"And *where* is home this week?"

Mrs. Pierce, the school administrative assistant, asked him this.

His brain blistered.

"Your parents didn't fill out the multiple-residence sheet that we sent to them in the fall. We need to know where you are, and when, for emergencies."

She handed him a form with multiple boxes for two home addresses, two business addresses, faxes, e-mails, cell phones, beepers.

He handed her the monthlong schedule his mother had given him—color-coordinated for each week (yellow for when he would be living with her, blue for when he would be living with his father).

When life got tough, his mother got organized.

Mrs. Pierce looked at the schedule. "Will this be changing monthly?"

He shifted. "Yes."

"You'll be getting a new schedule monthly?" She had a too-loud voice.

He nodded.

"You'll need to bring that by the office on the first of the month. *And* we need to know who is the custodial parent—your mother or father."

"They're doing it together even though they're divorced." He said this quietly.

"If your parents are co-custodians, then that's a different form."

She handed him that form.

"Is there one parent who should be contacted with all school issues?"

He sighed. "They kind of take turns."

She handed him a form for that. "If *both* parents want to be contacted on any issue, it makes it a little more difficult for us. If they *both* want to receive your report cards, we need to know that, too."

He didn't want anyone to receive his report cards. He wished there was a form for that.

Mr. Cosgrove, the school janitor, was fixing a squeaky door. He took out his little can of oil, squirted a few drops in the hinges. Opened it, closed it. Instantly fixed.

Mr. Cosgrove could fix anything.

"Is there anything else?" Mrs. Pierce shoved her reading glasses low on her nose.

He wondered if oil worked on administrative assistants.

"Oh, yes," she snipped. "*Who* will be receiving the invoice for school trips?"

She gazed up at him, way up.

He bent his knees to seem shorter.

"I don't know," he said.

"That can be put on this form—form C—which you can attach to form D, which covers any emergency medical care you might require when you are off school property but participating in school activities, like athletics. And if *both* your parents want to receive an audiocassette of the principal's nondenominational holiday address, they need to put an X in that box. I think that's it. The newsletter comes out quarterly and can also be mailed to grandparents and other interested parties."

"My grandpa lives with my dad."

"That saves us on postage. I'll need those back by Friday."

He looked at the forms in his hand.

There it was in black and white, just how complicated his life had become.

He stood in front of the huge white oak tree in the middle of Ripley Memorial Park. It was tall and thick with serious bark.

An oak with attitude.

He cocked his head, stretched his long arms out, imitating the tree, and froze.

He'd seen a street performer do this in New York City—the man drew a big crowd. Every so often the man would move slightly. People put money in his hat.

Mrs. Clitter walked by with her granddaughter and stopped.

He didn't move, didn't breathe.

They looked up at him for the longest time.

He moved his right hand a little.

Then his left.

The little girl giggled.

Mrs. Clitter said, "Now, where'd you learn to do that?"

He said nothing. Part of the act.

Winked at the little girl, who grinned.

He had an itch, but didn't scratch it. Mrs. Clitter moved off, laughing. He lifted his leg slightly, wiggled it.

"You say a big hello to that grandfather of yours," she shouted. Mrs. Clitter was in love with his grandfather. "You tell him I'm going to do everything I know to do to help him in his time of need." His grandfather, currently in the Veterans Administration Hospital in Baltimore, had his right leg removed just below the knee two weeks ago. His grandfather usually hid when he saw Mrs. Clitter coming. This was harder to do with half a leg, but he was working on it.

The little girl waved good-bye and crossed the bridge with her grandmother.

He straightened to full height—six feet, three and a half inches.

He was the tallest seventh-grade boy in the history of Eleanor Roosevelt Middle School.

The tallest twelve-year-old boy anyone in Ripley had ever seen.

Now you know why people called him Tree.

It had been years since anyone had called him by his real name, Sam. Jeremy Liggins had first called him Tree in fourth grade. Jeremy was one of those emperor athletes who got to do whatever he wanted. He'd stood on the baseball diamond and

4

renamed half the class, like Adam named the animals in the Bible.

Jeremy's friends got the cool names.

Fire.

Boomerang.

When it came to nonathlete nobodies, the names got harder.

Tree.

Mole.

Snot.

He'd gotten used to the name. Considered the white oak.

Some of its roots protruded from the ground—fat roots that wound around rocks.

He had studied the root systems of trees. Figured if he was going to be called one, he should at least know how they worked.

He'd learned this from his grandfather, who could fix almost anything except Tree's parents' marriage. "You've got to take a thing apart to see what it's made of," his grandpa always said.

So he learned how roots could go as deep in the ground as a tree's branches grow tall.

How they suck up nutrients from the earth like a boy slurps a milk shake through a straw. How the bark protects the tree's insides like skin protects people.

How being a tree is the best thing going in the plant world. People expect trees to be strong and steady and give good shade.

Tallness is packed with great expectations.

He picked up his duffel bag, remembered what he'd forgotten to pack.

Now that he was living every other week at different houses, he always forgot to pack something.

His warm gloves were at his mother's house.

His good sneakers were, too. He needed them for basketball practice, but it would take a lot more than sneakers to make him good at the game.

He couldn't remember if he packed underwear.

Probably not.

His personal park squirrel, Nuts, came a foot away to greet him. Nuts had half an ear, so he was easy to spot. He was more nervous than the other squirrels. Tree always wondered what happened to him. A dysfunctional childhood, probably.

"Hey, Nuts." Tree took out a bag of almonds, tossed one to the squirrel. "How's life in the park?"

Nuts shook a little, ate the food.

"You being treated okay? Because if anything's hassling you, you give me a call."

He threw the squirrel another nut.

A strong, cold wind whipped through the park. He'd been playing here, walking here for so many years. But since his parents got divorced, it felt like a different place.

Up the stairs to the north was where he'd go when he was staying at his mom's new house.

Across the footbridge to the south was where his dad and grandfather still lived.

So much had changed since the summer.

Including the white oak.

Its fat green leaves had turned red in the fall, then shriveled up. The acorns had fallen off, picked up by squirrels getting ready for winter.

It was winter in his life, too, and not just because it was December.

He started walking toward his father's house, past a lone Salvation Army trumpeter playing Christmas carols. Fished in his pocket, found a dollar, put it in the red bucket.

Mrs. Stench's dog, Fang, trotted toward him, barking mean.

"Fang, be nice." Mrs. Stench yanked on the expanding leash, lurched forward.

Fang ran up to the white oak, lifted his leg, and peed on the noble gray bark.

Tree sighed deep; cold air came out.

Being a tree isn't easy.

CHAPTER TWO

Tree sat at the computer in his father's dining room.

Typed in *heymom.com.*

Up on the screen came the smiling face of his mother. A bouncing bird flitted across a cloud that read *Thought for the day.*

The cloud morphed into *Divorce ended our marriage, but our loving family will never end.*

This was a big theme that Tree's parents were trying to get across.

A little Christmas tree appeared on the screen. An elf was underneath it.

19 Days Till Christmas appeared over the tree. *I can't wait.* The elf giggled.

Tree sighed.

This would be the first Christmas since the divorce.

The computer screen flickered.

Up popped his mother's schedule. She was in Boston for three days teaching computer seminars, but she was reachable by beeper, cell phone, and e-mail for anything he needed.

He pictured his mother beeping, ringing, and whirring all at once.

Remembered all the hours she put in when she was going to school to become a computer whiz. She'd sit at this machine, working late into the night.

Went from teaching aerobics to running computer seminars in three and a half years. Once his mom got interested in something, she'd learn everything about it that she could.

She'd done that with divorce, too.

A letter from his mother appeared on the screen.

Dear Curtis, Larry, and Tree, it began.

Curtis and Larry were his big brothers, both away at college.

I've been collecting thoughts about Christmas. I'd like us to talk about our feelings in the midst of so much change.

Tree didn't like talking about his feelings.

A wreath came up on the screen.

Then the words: *Change is part of life. It is the healthy family that learns to adapt to change that prepares each member for our ever-changing, complex world.*

And here's the first question we can discuss. **How are we all feeling this Christmas season?**

In the response section was a three-word reply from Larry, a freshman at Penn State.

I've got gas, Larry wrote.

Tree started laughing. He could see his mother's smile getting tight when she read that.

Very funny, she'd replied. *Humor is one of the ways to diffuse feelings of alienation and frustration at the holidays.*

Then up on the screen was a response from his brother Curtis, a sophomore at the University of New Hampshire.

I've got more gas than you.

Tree really laughed now. He knew his mom was trying to reach out, but how she did it sometimes was hard.

His mother wrote, *It's certainly nice you're learning such cogent ways of communicating at college. It's certainly nice that you've bothered to respond at all.*

Tree tried to think of what he could write back. He ate some barbecue potato chips, burped twice. Maybe *I've got more gas than anybody.*

Tree really broke up at this and wished his best friend, Sully Devo, was here. Sully had the best laugh of anyone Tree knew. Sully would laugh so hard, he'd fall off a chair and say, "You're killing me, you're killing me," then he'd pull himself together, sit down, and start cracking up all over again.

He clicked on the elf. "Deck the Halls" began to play in that computer-generated musical way.

He shut the computer down. Watched his mother's cyber self disappear from the screen.

On-line quality time, she called it.

He looked at the empty wall where the big hutch used to be.

His mother had taken it when she moved out. The shadows of where it had been remained. His dad said they were going to get a new hutch, but they hadn't yet.

His dad said they were going to repaint the downstairs so the darkened places on the walls where the pictures had hung—the ones his mother took when she moved out—would be gone.

10

They hadn't done that, either.

Divorce casts so many shadows.

Tree and his brothers had helped her move out.

Their old dog, Bradley, kept going up to Tree's mother to get rubbed, and every time he did, she'd start to cry. Bradley tried to climb in the U-Haul truck, but Tree's father dragged him back into the house.

Tree's grandpa spoke for everyone: "My God, Jan, I'm going to miss you like crazy."

It was like a sci-fi movie where someone is there one minute, gone the next.

Poof.

Curtis said he'd seen the breakup coming.

Larry knew Mom was going to leave Dad, too.

Tree sure hadn't. It was like watching floodwaters burst through a dam he'd always expected to hold.

Tree tried to understand how his parents went from seeming okay, but kind of bored and crabby, to living in different houses.

They'd waited to get divorced until Larry had gone to college.

Why hadn't they waited for Tree to go, too?

He stretched his long legs out. His muscles were sore, which meant he was growing more.

He wondered when he'd stop. He'd been wondering that for years.

In first grade when he sat on a stool for the class picture while the other kids stood around him.

In second grade when Mr. Cosgrove had to add another panel to the "How Tall Am I?" poster just for him.

In third grade when he got stuck in a desk and Mr. Cosgrove had to pry him out.

In fourth grade when he played a kind tree in the school play and no one had to sit on his shoulders to be the branches.

In fifth grade when he was Frankenstein at the Women's Auxiliary's House of Horrors and scared Timmy Bigelow's sister so bad, she peed in her pants.

In sixth grade when he was taller than his teachers and the principal.

And this year, seventh grade, when he just sat in the back at the table because he was too big for the desks.

The back table wasn't so bad.

Bradley padded over, put his paw in Tree's hand. Bradley understood when people needed comfort. The older and slower Bradley got, the more he seemed to know.

"Good dog."

Tree scratched Bradley's head, massaged his neck like the vet showed him.

"We've got to practice your trick."

Tree walked into the kitchen, Bradley followed. Tree got out a large dog biscuit from the canister.

"Bradley, sit."

Bradley sat.

"Good dog."

Tree got the picture he'd drawn of a sitting dog balancing a biscuit on his nose. He showed it to Bradley, who looked at it. Tree had invented this method of dog training.

"Okay, that's what you're going to do. Ready?"

Tree balanced the biscuit on Bradley's nose, put his hand out in the stay command. Bradley sat still, balancing it, as Tree timed him with his watch.

People think you can't teach an old dog new tricks, but an old dog is going to pay attention when you're doing something serious.

After forty-five seconds, the biscuit dropped, Bradley ate it.

"Good dog."

He made Bradley his dinner, put it on the floor. He made two serious submarine sandwiches with extra meat and cheese, put them in a bag.

A car horn outside.

"That's my ride, Bradley. I've got to go see Grandpa."

Bradley looked up, wagged his tail.

Seeing Grandpa was the best part of the week for just about anybody.

CHAPTER THREE

"Is that man behaving himself or being difficult?"

Mrs. Clitter half shouted the question over the phone.

Tree held the receiver, looked at his grandfather lying in the hospital bed at the VA with half a leg all bandaged up. The VA is a special hospital for people who've served in the military.

"She wants to know if you're behaving yourself."

"Tell her I'm dead."

"Grandpa . . ." Tree covered the receiver.

"Tell her I have amnesia."

"She'll come and take care of you."

"Tell her I escaped." He motioned for Tree to hang up.

Tree sighed, phone to his ear. "He's behaving. But he's got to get some sleep, Mrs. Clitter."

"Let me just say good night."

Tree extended the phone. Grandpa shook his head, made snoring noises.

Tree: "He's already asleep, ma'am."

"You tell him I'll call in the morning."

Tree hung up the phone.

Grandpa raised a tired hand. "That woman needs a hobby."

"Sounds like she's got one," said Wild Man Finzolli, Grandpa's roommate. *"You."*

A loud groan from the old soldier.

Tree scrunched down in the vinyl chair that had been designed by a short person, rearranged his body to get comfortable.

Sometimes it seemed like the whole world had been designed by people shorter than him.

Airplane seats were misery.

Mattresses were never long enough.

Regular clothes didn't fit—he had to shop at the Big Guy Shop in Baltimore.

Regular shoes were out—he had to order from the Big Foot catalog.

The pediatrician had run tests to see if Tree had some kind of condition that made him so tall, like Marfan's syndrome or giantism.

He didn't.

"You're just unusually large," Dr. Flemmer said, like that explained it.

Tree shoved his long legs out.

He couldn't imagine losing a leg.

A young nurse came in to change Grandpa's bandage. "How are you, Mr. Benton?"

"It's getting harder for me to sneak up on people."

She laughed, unrolled the bandages down to the stump. Tree didn't want to look, but he did. The leg stump looked better than it had the first day—a big raw wound with staples. It still looked pretty angry.

But his grandfather wasn't into bellyaching.

Hadn't been since the Vietnam War, when his leg got shot up with shrapnel when he was on a night patrol in the Mekong Delta. There had been multiple surgeries to try and fix it, but like the Vietnam War, that leg just wouldn't behave.

"Take it off," Grandpa finally said to his doctor. "It's more trouble than it's worth."

And the long road back to healing began.

First, he'd be in a wheelchair.

Then, he'd get around with a walker.

Months later, he'd be fitted for a prosthetic leg—a leg specially made to take the place of the old one.

Tree's grandfather wanted that new leg bad.

The nurse put on a fresh bandage and left.

Grandpa slid to the end of the bed, sat up. His arms were strong. He nodded to Tree, who brought the walker over.

They'd been practicing this.

Good leg on the floor.

"Lean on me, Grandpa."

He did. Tree took the weight. If there was ever a reason to be a too-tall seventh-grader, it was so you could help your grandpa get walking again.

Tree's grandpa steadied himself as Tree held on tight to the walker. Slowly, Grandpa moved it forward.

"Awright, Leo," Wild Man shouted. "Reach for the stars."

"I lost my leg, Finzolli, not my arm."

Slow moving to the door and back. Grandpa plopped down on the bed.

"That's a couple miles, right?"

"At least," Tree said, smiling.

Grandpa grinned back. "You want to take apart an ugly lamp and make it uglier?"

Tree really wanted to do that.

He got the trunk out from under the bed, opened it to his grandfather's tools of the trade—pliers, wires, sockets, plugs. Grandpa was a master electrician who repaired lamps in his workshop above the garage. He'd brought this to the hospital so he wouldn't go crazy.

They worked for two hours, not counting the time it took to eat the two submarine sandwiches and the two bags of barbecue potato chips Tree had brought with him. They took the lamp apart, laid the pieces on the bed, examined the insides. Talked about how the wires had been broken and the power couldn't get to the bulb.

"When that happens, nothing works," Grandpa said. "Kind of like life."

They glued nails around the base. Grandpa searched in the trunk, held up a rubber tarantula.

"I've been saving this bug for the finishing touch." He hung it off the lamp's side.

They rigged up a little motor that rotated the lamp and shot the tarantula's shadow against the wall in creepy red light.

It was the best lamp in the universe.

"That," said Belle, the night nurse, "is *disgusting*."

Tree was so proud.

Disgusting is what they were going for.

Belle folded her arms across her chest. "You're not supposed to have tools in the room, Leo. You know that."

"Belle, I'm saving you grief. Let me tinker around here, or I'll get so bored, I'll start taking this hospital apart piece by piece."

"Someone already beat you to it," shouted Wild Man, looking at the peeling paint, the broken TV.

Tree couldn't wait for his grandpa to come home.

Tree's father was late picking him up at the hospital. He'd never been too punctual, but since the divorce, he was so late for everything.

Tree's mother had been the time sheriff.

It was one of the things Tree's parents always fought about.

Nine P.M. Visiting hours had been over for a half hour. Tree was getting nervous that something had happened to his dad.

Things made him more nervous these days.

At nine-thirty, a nurse going off duty said Tree had to leave.

Tree got really upset at that.

"Put on one of those patient robes," Grandpa told him. "Those awful things that flop open in the back. Sit on the empty bed and look wounded."

Tree did this, feeling strange. A hospital attendant came in at ten, stared at Tree. "I don't remember you here before."

"He just got transferred," Grandpa explained.

"Where's his chart?"

"On its way up," said Wild Man.

Tree slumped his shoulders, tried to look wounded.

The attendant walked closer. "Where'd you come from, soldier?"

Tree tried to think of a recent war and couldn't, so he said, "Canada."

The attendant looked surprised. "Canada?"

"It was a secret mission," Grandpa said.

"It saved the Republic," Wild Man whispered.

Tree tried to look brave and humble.

"This one's got some stories to tell," Grandpa added.

Tree sniffed. "I got a few." He'd heard a cowboy say that in a movie once.

Then, thankfully, the attendant's beeper went off and he headed for another room.

His grandpa gave him a thumbs-up; Wild Man said he seemed so much like a real soldier, he could have fooled a five-star general.

A regular-sized kid couldn't have pulled that off.

Tree's father rushed into the room like he'd driven a hundred miles an hour to get there.

"Sorry. There was a problem with the computer at the store, we had a shoplifter, my best checker quit."

He managed a sporting goods store, or maybe it managed him.

He looked at Grandpa. "How you doing, Pop?"

19

"They're going to paint my stump green for Christmas so we don't have to look at the purple lines anymore."

He laughed. "That's good, Pop."

He looked at Tree in the robe.

"What's this?"

"I saved the Republic," Tree explained, and went into the bathroom to get dressed.

"Hold this here, Dad."

They were in the bathroom of their house, putting up rails around the toilet so Grandpa would have something to hold on to when he came home.

Father and son looked at each other, wondered how the other was doing.

"You okay?" Dad asked, looking up. Tree's father was five-eleven.

Tree nodded.

"Good." Dad slapped Tree's back, relieved.

He so wanted Tree to be okay. To look at this boy, it was easy to believe he was handling things.

How could someone so big not be fine?

"You okay, Dad?"

Weak smile. "I'm just tired. Christmas, you know."

Tree knew.

Christmas for retailers was crazy—the late hours, the difficult customers.

But Tree's dad was tired down deep.

He tried to explain it with sports.

"All this change, Tree, is kind of like trying to bat left-handed when you've been a righty all your life."

Tree mostly struck out. He could barely bat right-handed, much less left.

"Divorce is like being in the fourth quarter with ten seconds left on the clock. They throw the ball to you and you get pushed back from the goal. You can't make it over. You don't make the play-offs."

Tree had always been one of those linemen anyone could get by—even a small child—but he knew that not making the play-offs was a bad thing.

Curtis and Larry were athletes. They spoke Dad's language.

Tree wanted to speak it, too. "It's like you don't get your contract renewed. Right, Dad? You get sent to the minors."

"Not *exactly.* . . ."

Dad went to bed.

Getting ready for bed, watching the clock tick off the seconds, minutes. On Saturday, Tree had taken the clock apart to see how it was made, and when he put it back together, there were two parts left on the table. He didn't trust the clock much after that.

He got into his queen-size bed, lay at an angle, covered himself with two blankets. Angle sleeping gave him more room.

He had heard that people grow when they sleep, so last year he'd tried to stay awake to stop his bones from expanding. He was so tired, he kept tripping over Bradley, who up to that time had felt safe sleeping in the hall.

A cold draft blew into the room. He hadn't minded a drafty room as much when his parents were still married, but his room seemed colder these days.

He tried to sleep. Couldn't.

Got out the cool laser pen his father had gotten him from the sporting goods show at the convention center.

Took out the insides. Put each part on the desk. Studied the laser section—it was so small to make such a big light.

There was a beauty in seeing how things worked, machines in particular.

Grandpa taught him that.

He put the pen back together piece by piece, saw the clean lines of each ink cartridge, the small tunnel for the laser beam that had to be fixed on the little battery just so. The batteries had to be put in the right way or the flashlight wouldn't work. There was no other road to take in the battery world—the negative and positive ends had to be touching.

He turned out the light and shone the laser on the wall, making circles and slashes like a space warrior.

He wished life could be simple like a laser pen—with clean lines and a clear purpose.

Chapter Four

"Men..."

Coach Glummer walked slowly across the basketball court in the Eleanor Roosevelt Middle School gym and studied the faces of his team, the Fighting Pit Bulls.

"What, men, is the purpose of basketball?"

This seemed like a trick question to Tree. Most of his school day had been filled with them.

What is the purpose of an adverb?

Why is grammar important?

Who was the thirty-second president of the United States?

Coach Glummer looked for an upturned face. "Darkus?"

Steven Darkus, who was as bad at basketball as Tree, took a wild stab. "To make the basket?"

"That's it, Darkus. The purpose of basketball, the purpose of this team, is to make the basket again and again. We have failed in that purpose—with two exceptions."

The exceptions were Jeremy Liggins and Raul Cosada, the best players.

He walked past the team. Stopped by the plaque the PTA put up after last year's pitiful season—words of encouragement from Eleanor Roosevelt herself:

No one can make you feel inferior without your consent.

Coach Glummer had always felt that Eleanor Roosevelt, a tall person, had untapped basketball potential.

"There is hidden talent on this team, and we're going to find it." He stood in front of Tree and gazed up.

"There's gold in you, kid."

"There's not, Coach. Really."

"You're a Pit Bull for a reason."

The *reason*, thought Tree, is that I need six sports credits to graduate from middle school.

Coach Glummer put the ball in Tree's huge hands. "I know talent when I see it."

And Tree so wanted to tell him that being big didn't mean being talented. Being big didn't mean extra special or superhuman or athletically gifted.

It just meant large.

Every coach Tree had ever known believed that somewhere he had athletic ability.

"Keep your eye on the ball," coaches had shouted to him over the years.

Tree tried. He focused on basketballs, footballs, baseballs, golf balls, soccer balls, tennis balls, Ping-Pong balls, but they rarely went where they were supposed to go.

"Trust your instincts," they told him.

Tree tried. But his basic instinct was to avoid sports altogether.

"Use your strength," they'd advise.

Tree knew he was strong, but he couldn't figure out how to use it. He could lift a couch by himself, but that didn't come in handy except when his mother was rearranging the furniture.

"Keep practicing," they'd shout.

Tree kept practicing and stayed mediocre.

"I'm not real athletic," he told coach after coach.

But they weren't listening. They were remembering the trophy years when Tree's brothers, Curtis and Larry, carried their teams to victory.

Tree's father came back from those games a proud man. Curtis and Larry got college sports scholarships.

Tree's dad came back from Tree's games saying, "It's not about winning, it's about playing your best."

That's what winning athletes always say to losers.

Tree hoped there were college scholarships for height.

He wished Coach Glummer could see him help his grandfather. He could steady a one-hundred-and-eighty-pound man by himself, fold up and carry a wheelchair one-handed, but that didn't count on the basketball court or in grammar or much of anywhere.

He bounced the basketball in his hands.

Bounced it again.

Mr. Cosgrove was fixing the scoreboard.

Someone had taken some letters off again. Instead of PIT BULLS it read PITS.

Last week it read BULL PITS.

Mr. Cosgrove stood on a tall ladder, added the BULL, moved the S, epoxied them in place. Held them down till the glue set. Those letters weren't going anywhere.

Nothing like epoxy to make a thing right.

Tree bounced the ball, kept his eye on the net. Shot.

Missed.

He tried five times.

Coach Glummer shouted, *"You're so close to the net, kid, how can you keep missing?"*

Because, Tree thought, *I'm not good at this.*

Mr. Cosgrove walked off, carrying his ladder; smiled so kindly at Tree. Just last week, he'd fixed the door in the library—rescued Mrs. Asher, the librarian, who'd been stuck in the media center for two hours.

Jeremy Liggins made an easy basket, smirked at Tree.

Tree wanted to make baskets, too, but even more than that, he wanted to go home.

"There are big things in store for you, boy." Tree's uncle Roger always told him this. *"Big* things."

What are they?

That's what Tree wanted to know.

VA Rehab Center. Six P.M.

Grandpa was tired, but he wasn't going to admit it. He stood at the parallel bars. There were mirrors all around. Tree put a riser in front of him. Dad was supposed to be here tonight, but there'd been a problem at the store again.

Mona Arnold, the physical therapist, wore a white jacket

and white pants. She'd been born in Ethiopia in eastern Africa, came here as a girl.

She stood alongside Grandpa. "Learning to move without that leg is going to feel different than when you were walking with an injured one, Leo. Our brains are wired to have all our limbs working. I want you to take it slow and not be a hotshot."

"Check."

Grandpa didn't like going slow. He grabbed the bars, slid forward, up on the riser and down again. Over and over. Tree watched.

"That's good, Leo. How does that feel?"

"Like the leg's still there and hurting."

He'd have sworn last night it had never gotten amputated at all.

Mona nodded. "That's called phantom pain. It's very normal."

Grandpa muttered that it might be normal, but it sure felt weird having a ghost for a leg.

"The big goal," she said to Tree, "is to get your grandpa strong so he can get his new leg. I need to teach him how to do things with half a leg that lots of people take for granted. Getting on the toilet. Taking a bath. Getting dressed. Getting in and out of a car, maneuvering around the kitchen, carrying food from one room to the next. The more you understand how this works, Tree, the more you can help."

Tree nodded, brought the walker over. Grandpa wheeled himself to an exercise pad, hopping on his good leg. Tree helped him lie down, strapped a leg weight to his stump.

Other men were exercising, too.

"Lift, Leo," Mona said. "Hold it for eight."

Grandpa struggled with this.

Luger, a huge vet who'd lost a hand, was practicing holding a cup with a prosthetic hand. He kept dropping the cup. Over and over he tried to pick it up.

"You almost got it, Luger," a soldier in a back brace shouted.

"How's that leg feel, Leo?" Mona asked.

"Like I've got a lead weight attached to a sore stump. You're a cruel woman."

She smiled. "I get meaner. Three reps on that. Then switch to your good leg. Five reps. We've got to strengthen the good leg because it's going to be taking more of the weight. All through this process we're going to strengthen the best you've got. So, what have you got, Leo?"

Grandpa looked at his half leg. It was easy to see the loss of it. He was a one-legged man; disabled.

But he wasn't going to concentrate on that.

"I've got every part of my body working except below my right knee. I've got a decent mind, a big-time stubborn streak, and a world-class grandson."

Tree smiled bright.

"That's a lot, Leo."

A few more reps, Grandpa switched the weight to his good leg. This was hard work.

Luger dropped the cup again, frustrated. He'd been a drummer. He sure couldn't do that now.

He shouted out like a drill sergeant, "*Men,* are we having fun yet?"

"No, sir!" the vets cried out.

"*Men*, are we going to fight this like soldiers or fools?"

The vets looked at one another, grinned.

"Like fools, sir!"

Everyone laughed.

Luger dropped his cup again, but this time he kicked it hard across the room.

"*I can still kick!*"

And everyone in rehab worked a little harder.

Tree took it in, thinking about his oral report he had to give tomorrow on the Vietnam War.

Tree hated oral reports.

Jeremy Liggins smirked at him, made him forget things. Once Jeremy held up a sign when Tree was giving a report on wolves.

BEHEMOTH BOY, it read.

Tree forgot a whole section of his report that day.

"Gargantuan Gargoyle"—that was Jeremy's latest name for Tree.

Tree took the names apart. Decided Jeremy had his species confused—he could be either a boy or a gargoyle, not both.

Tree wasn't going to look at Jeremy tomorrow.

He'd look at Sully, who would seem interested even if he was bored stiff. Sully wore a hearing aid and *never* turned it off when Tree was giving a report.

That's the kind of friend he was.

Tree had never worked so hard on a report in his life.

He hoped he could change Mr. Pender's C-minus opinion

of him as a public speaker. He always got a C minus from Mr. Pender.

"More energy, Tree." Mr. Pender always said this. "Make eye contact. Make that delivery snappy. Show us you care. Make *us* care."

CHAPTER FIVE

"What is the purpose of war?"

Tree said this loud to the class; tried to make eye contact, nervous as anything.

"Sometimes the answer is clear. In the Revolutionary War, the United States wanted freedom from taxation from England. In the Civil War, the country fought over slavery. In World War Two, countries came together to stop Hitler's invasion across Europe. But the Vietnam War was different. To many people, the purpose of that war is still unclear."

Tree felt his mouth get chalky; he looked at Mr. Pender, who actually looked interested. Sully leaned forward in his seat.

Tree turned to the first poster he'd made—showing antiwar demonstrations and soldiers fighting in the jungle.

"Our country was divided about Vietnam. Some people believed the war should go on and some people felt it was wrong. It was a new kind of war, too, because people could see it on their TV screens and watch people die in battle. It was a different kind of war because of the military weapons that were used."

Another poster. This one of unusual words.

"The Vietnam War had its own language. A 'Bird' was a plane. A 'Big Boy' was a tank. 'Bug Juice' was insect repellent."

The class laughed. Tree felt strong, way above C minus.

" 'Greased,' " Tree said solemnly, "meant killed."

He talked about the U.S. presidents who oversaw the war— Eisenhower, Kennedy, Johnson, Nixon, Ford. He talked about President Jimmy Carter, who gave amnesty to the draft dodgers, men who left the country instead of fighting in a war that they didn't think was right.

He talked about how so many vets felt like unwelcome strangers when they came home because the country had changed while they were gone.

He showed them pictures of the Vietnam Veterans Memorial in Washington, D.C., which had every name of every soldier who had died carved into a wall.

He talked about putting a wreath by his grandfather's good friend's name.

"When you go there, you can see your reflection in the black stone of the wall," Tree explained. "It makes us all part of the experience."

Tree held up a photo of Leo looking sharp in his uniform. "My grandfather served in Vietnam. He was wounded in battle. I asked him what he thought kids should know about the war."

Tree pressed PLAY on the tape recorder. Grandpa's voice boomed through the classroom.

"The people who went to fight that war, for the most part, did their best to fight an enemy that was harder to figure out and more dangerous than any of us knew. Most of us were kids—nineteen, twenty—I was twenty-five. We thought we'd kick butt and everything would be over fast. We'd win. We didn't win. I think we stayed too long and made some really bad mistakes. But we did things right, too. I think important things are worth fighting for, but there's nothing glorious about battle, nothing cool about holding a gun. It's scary and lonely, and too many people die young. Never be a person who wants war—hate it with everything you've got. But if you've got to fight to protect people, try to do your job the best you know how. Protecting people is the only reason to ever fight."

Everyone was quiet after hearing that, even Lucy Pulaski, who had the biggest mouth in the whole seventh grade.

Tree forgot the quote he was going to use at the end. So he just said, "That's my report."

Mr. Pender led the applause.

Sully whistled loud and Mr. Pender glared at him, but he kept clapping.

Jeremy Liggins yawned and stretched.

Tree sat back in his seat, shaking from the stress.

Glad it was over, proud he'd stood the test.

A

Fat and red. It sat there on Mr. Pender's evaluation sheet of Tree's report.

Tree felt like shouting.

Then the VA said Grandpa could come home on Friday.

What a great week.

Tree was going to make this the best homecoming ever for a Vietnam vet. Grandpa said he hadn't felt too welcome when he got back from the war.

"I was at the train station in my wheelchair, wearing my uniform," Grandpa had told him. "A woman stormed up to me and said, 'Was it worth it?' I didn't know what to say. She kept shouting that Vietnam was an unjust war; we had no business being there. She walked away like I smelled bad. I had plenty of friends who served and some who went to Canada to avoid the draft. But I've just learned to throw the circuit breaker on all that. Let the whole mess go dark."

Tree tucked his right knee back and hopped through Dad's kitchen as Bradley followed, confused. He was remembering what Mona Arnold had told him.

"Think about everything you do each day, and then think about doing it with a disability."

It was hard to hop in the house without falling.

Sully was at the dining room table, researching sedimentary rocks on the computer for their earth science report. Sully looked up. "What are you doing?"

Tree made it to a chair, eased himself down like Mona Arnold was teaching Grandpa to do.

"Butt down and slide," she instructed.

Butt sliding was a big part of rehab.

"That's what my grandpa's got to do when he gets home, Sully."

Sully nodded. He didn't know what it was like to have half

a leg, but he knew what it was like to have bad hearing. You have to try harder to understand what people are saying; watch what they do, not just what they say. Sully adjusted his hearing aid.

Tree looked around the room, thinking.

Homecomings should be fun.

He saw it in his mind. The best ideas are simple.

He grabbed a piece of paper, drew a clothesline on a pulley hung from the kitchen to the living room. A big basket suspended from the line, delivering food to wherever his grandpa was sitting.

Sully glared at the computer screen. "Who cares if sediment is mechanical, chemical, or organic? Knowing this will not help us later in life."

"Unless we drill for oil. I'll be right back."

Tree raced through the kitchen, into the garage, past the bikes and the lawn mower, past the old Chinese gong that used to hang on the back porch. His mother would ram it with a mallet to call him and his brothers in for dinner.

That sound shook the neighborhood.

It was out of commission now, like a warship in dry dock.

On a shelf he found a pulley, an old clothesline.

He grabbed his tool kit, too, ran back inside. Lugged forty feet of line past Sully, who shouted, "*What* are you doing?"

Tree was on a step stool, pulling rope through the pulley, when Dad came home with Chinese food.

"I can explain," Tree said. He and Sully tugged on the rope to make sure it was tight.

"Good." Dad stared at the clothesline stretched from kitchen to dining room.

"Dad, do we need the hanging lamp in the living room?"

"I'm kind of fond of it." Dad speared a dumpling with a chopstick.

"Can I just try something?"

"You should let him, Mr. Benton. This is more educational than homework."

Dad raised an eyebrow.

Tree took the hanging lamp off the hook, handed it down.

He fastened the pulley to the hook. Checked the weight, balance. "Grandpa won't be able to reach it here. It's got to be lower. Untie the rope, Dad."

Dad walked over, chewing, untied it.

"If I bolt it on the beam, Dad, it will be steady. Okay?"

Dad laughed. "I'm a sport."

"This is going to be so cool, Mr. Benton."

Bolt screwed in, pulley and rope adjusted.

Dad watched, smiling.

Tree ran to the kitchen, stuck a package of Mallomars in a basket, clamped the basket on the rope.

"This is how we can deliver food to Grandpa when he gets home, Dad."

Swoosh.

Tree pulled the rope through the pulley. The basket made a low loop in the dining room—he'd have to fix that—Bradley tucked his tail low and slinked away. The basket stopped right over the couch.

Bradley barked.

Tree beamed.

Dad grabbed it, laughing. "Terrific!"

Sully gazed respectfully at the invention. "My mother would croak if we tried that at my house."

Tree and Dad nodded.

Occasionally something awful, like divorce, can have a good side.

It was late. Dad was asleep.

Tree stood in the driveway in front of the basketball hoop. The air was cold; his breath rose like steam.

He bounced the ball.

Tried to rise up on his toes like Curtis taught him.

Took a shot.

Missed.

Another.

Almost.

He dribbled the ball up and down the driveway.

The neighbors couldn't see how bad he was at night.

He wasn't graceful like Curtis, who could dribble a ball past anyone to make the basket.

He wasn't easy with himself like Larry, who could pick up a bat and hit a home run on the first pitch.

He wondered why he was not like his brothers.

Curtis and Larry were coming home on Friday, too.

Curtis took time to do things with Tree. They'd play basketball together. And unlike his coaches, who always told Tree what he was doing wrong, Curtis shouted out what he was doing right.

"Good move on the hands."

"Good bounce on the ball."

"Good focus, you almost had that basket."

Larry was a pain. "Giant tree sloth," that's what he called Tree.

Tree tried to take the insult apart, find the good. *Giant* he could live with, but *sloth* didn't have an up side.

He got out the can of deicer, sprayed the front steps, watched the ice evaporate. The ice had to be gone so Grandpa wouldn't fall when he came home.

He wondered if deicer would work on Larry.

Then he remembered.

Everyone was coming home, but he was supposed to stay at his mom's next week.

Curtis and Larry got to stay at Dad's for their whole winter break. Mom was supposed to turn her attic into a bedroom for them, but she couldn't yet. Money was tight.

Tree threw the can down.

He *had* to be there when Grandpa and his brothers came home.

Chapter Six

Tree's mother . . .

In workout clothes.

At the kitchen counter.

Typing on her laptop computer while studying fabric swatches for the couch.

Looking up occasionally to make eye contact with Tree.

Uttered the Big Question: "Honey, what would you like most to happen on Christmas Day?"

What Tree wanted most was for it to be the way it had always been.

He didn't know how to say that.

The Christmas Schedule: "Your dad and I have worked it out. You and your brothers are going to be there for Christmas Eve, and then early in the morning he'll bring you all over here."

There and here.

It sounded so easy when she said it.

"I'm going to make apple, pecan, and pumpkin pies and

roast beef and get those dinner rolls you like. The tree will be up and it's going to be okay, honey. It's going to be fine."

Tree looked down.

He wasn't sure about *fine*. He knew it was going to be different.

A blur of memories flooded Tree:

Grandpa's Christmas lights strung around his house in Baltimore—the house looked like Santa Claus himself lived inside.

The blinking sign on the roof—MERRY CHRISTMAS, EVERYONE!

The crowds walking by.

Bradley's reindeer outfit that one year. *Bad* idea.

The Christmas the stove broke and they had to eat at that all-you-can-eat buffet.

The Christmas Larry threw up on their grandmother's lace tablecloth and they finally figured out he was allergic to turkey.

The Christmas Mom broke her leg and lay on the couch, shouting instructions for *where* each ornament was to be hung properly on the tree.

Mom had stopped typing. "If I could, honey, I would fast-forward us all to a few years down the road when we'll be more comfortable with this, even though I'd be older." She laughed, looked at the fabric swatches on her lap. "Green, I think. Stripes get tired."

Tree didn't understand how stripes could get tired.

His mother used mysterious words when she decorated.

"Curtis and Larry are coming home on Friday," he said.

She smiled. "I know." She was clipping coupons now.

"Grandpa's coming home then, too."

She looked up. "So soon?"

Big breath. "And, Mom, you know, I promised I'd help when Grandpa got home. He's going to need a lot of help."

She knew that. She loved Leo, too.

"It's not that I don't want to be here." He looked down; didn't like lying.

"It's just that you want to be *there*," she said flatly.

She wished she hadn't said it that way.

"I'll come visit, Mom. I promise."

She threw down the coupons. "I don't *ever* want you to feel like you're just visiting me. I'm doing everything I can to make this house our home."

Tree looked at the freshly painted light green walls.

The yellow curtains at the windows.

The scented dried flowers that would make his father sneeze.

Conan, the little gray terrier she got after the divorce, was barking with irritation.

"I'll let him out, Mom."

"He's just saying hi."

Conan looked like he wanted to kill someone.

Mom smiled weakly. "Hi, baby. Hi."

Tree tried to feel at home, but there weren't any memories here.

The rooms were cramped, the ceilings were low, the dog was too small.

He'd walk through the door and divorce would hit him in the face.

He stood up, cracked his head on the low-hanging ceiling light.

"Oh, honey." His mom checked the cut. "Let me put something on that."

The pain stung.

She dabbed the cut with cotton and peroxide.

He didn't know the house well enough to remember where to duck.

Ducking is a key survival skill for the too tall.

Tree and Conan were standing in Ripley Memorial Park in front of the great white oak. Conan didn't appreciate this tree like Bradley, who would lie down in front of it in dog reverence. People said this oak had been there close to two hundred years. Just growing all that time.

Trees never stop growing; he'd read that somewhere.

To most people, that's an interesting fact. To him, it was grim news.

"We're going to have to raise the roof if you get any taller," Uncle Roger always said.

Having to raise the roof was one of Tree's greatest fears.

He touched the wound on his head, remembered the story Grandpa told him about the USS *Constitution,* a battleship. The ship had been made from wood of the white oak. That wood was so hard, cannonballs bounced off it during battles at sea.

Old Ironsides, the boat got named.

Tree would like to be made of such tough stuff.

His grandpa sure was.

No matter what happened to him, he kept on going.

When his wife died of cancer seven years ago.

When he had to sell his electrical business because his leg got so bad.

Tree had heard the big story so often—the one about Grandpa in the hospital in Vietnam when his leg had been shot.

So scared.

Sure that leg was going to go.

Men dying all around him.

"I wasn't strong enough to handle it," Grandpa said. "Then a chaplain came over, asked how I was doing. I told him. A nurse was calling him to come quick to the bed of a soldier hurt worse than me. But he grabbed my hand and said the shortest prayer: 'Lord, let this man's best years be ahead of him.' He ran to the other soldier's bed. But that prayer just stuck. I couldn't shake it. I got home a month later. I've never had much luck with the leg, but I say that prayer close to every day."

A cold wind blasted through the park. Tree pushed up his hood, shivered. Conan whimpered.

Tree took out the blue-and-yellow schedule his mother made for December.

Blue was for Bradley and Grandpa.

Yellow was for Conan the Crab.

Blue was when he got to feel real.

Yellow was when he didn't fit.

Curtis and Larry were too old to have plasticized sheets. Too old to be told where to go, where to sleep.

When you're twelve, everyone tells you where to go, what you need.

He wanted everything he cared about under one roof.

What Conan wanted was anybody's guess. This dog was barking weird.

"You want to walk some more?"

Conan wouldn't budge.

"You want me to rub you?"

Conan backed away.

"You want to be a famous, rich dog on television?"

Conan moaned, couldn't take the cold. Tree picked him up, stuffed him inside his coat, his little head sticking out, and walked back to his mother's house.

House.

He turned the word over in his mind.

I'm going to my house.

I'm going to my mother's house.

House was a word he'd always taken for granted.

He knew there was a big difference between a house and a home.

CHAPTER SEVEN

Mocha pecan frosted brownies wrapped in cellophane with a plaid bow. Sitting on Mom's kitchen counter.

Grandpa's favorite.

Tree knew she was going to let him stay at Dad's.

"Give these to Leo," Mom said. "I know this is an important week for all of you. I called your grandpa. We had a good talk. We hadn't talked for . . ." She started to cry, stopped herself.

"Thanks, Mom. I'll come and—" He was about to say *visit.* "I'll come over and tell you how everyone is doing and Curtis and Larry will come, too, and maybe Bradley even." He looked at Conan, who couldn't care less.

She touched his arm. "I know you have things to do to get ready."

"I love you, Mom."

"I love you, too."

He looked down; she looked up. She was five-nine.

He bent down to give her a hug. Took the brownies, almost dropped them.

Clutched the tray, walked carefully out the door.

He didn't see her fold her arms tight, lean against the refrigerator, and start to cry.

Curtis and Larry barreled into the house, tossed duffels in the hall.

"You look old enough to go, you might as well have one." Curtis threw a University of New Hampshire sweatshirt to Tree.

Tree put it on, beaming. "Thanks." Smiled at Larry, who looked upset. "Hi."

"Hi." Larry stood extra tall, didn't smile back. "Did you grow more?" Larry was five-eleven.

Tree shrugged. "Probably."

"You're the little brother now." Curtis laughed, poking Larry.

"Shut up," Larry snarled.

Curtis, six-one, looked at Tree: "How tall will he become? Stay tuned for the late-breaking news."

Tree slumped a little. "Come on, you guys."

Dad came racing home in the Kramer's Sports Mart van and they all headed to the VA to pick up Grandpa.

But Grandpa couldn't get in the van—it was too high.

Curtis and Larry tried to lift him. Grandpa cracked his head on the door.

"I'm going to need more surgery and I'm not home yet."

Tree, on hands and knees, a human step. Curtis and Larry lifted Grandpa up on Tree to the passenger seat. Curtis stepped on Tree's right hand. Larry stepped on Tree's left hand, and Tree shrieked right there in the hospital quiet zone.

"We're going to grab hold of the first rule of electrical power," Grandpa hollered. "You need a negative charge and a positive one to get something moving. We've got the negative; we're going to find the positive if it kills us."

Swoosh.

Tree had just put a submarine sandwich in the basket and let it ride to Grandpa in the living room. Curtis timed it.

"Thirteen and a half seconds," Curtis shouted.

Grandpa laughed. "You could earn money with this rig!" He pulled the rope from his end, shot the basket back. "You forgot the chips," he yelled.

Tree grabbed the basket that was racing toward him, stuck chips inside, hurled it back.

"I can get used to this," Grandpa shouted.

Curtis and Larry took over, trying to get the kitchen–to–living room run down to ten seconds.

Bradley stayed in the hall.

A knock on the door. Mrs. Clitter walked in, holding a basket; gave Grandpa a lovesick smile.

"Leo, this must be such a difficult time. I'm here to help in any way I can."

"Hello, Dorothy," he said miserably.

Swoosh.

She looked up, saw the ropes, the basket hurtling toward her.

"Duck," Grandpa ordered.

She did.

The basket flew by, stopped by Grandpa's arm.

"What *is* that?" Mrs. Clitter held her basket tight.

"State-of-the-art in-house food delivery by an up-and-coming genius." He sent the basket back.

Tree was so proud.

She stayed low. "I brought . . . *cookies.*"

"That's kind of you, Dorothy. You want to see my scar?"

"Actually—"

He leaned down to unroll the bandage. "It's still pretty ugly. It might be oozing pus or something worse."

"I'll come back later, Leo." She left the basket on the table, raced out the door.

Bradley barked.

Everyone laughed, ate the cookies.

Grandpa tried to get comfortable on the couch. Couldn't.

Tree could see the pain in his face.

"Are you okay?" Tree kept asking.

"I'm okay," he kept answering over the next few days as he did his exercises, practiced with his walker, strengthened the parts that were weak and were strong.

"How much time do I have left?"

Grandpa asked it, huffing and puffing on his exercise mat in the living room. He was doing his abdominal exercises twice a day like Mona Arnold told him.

Tree checked the stopwatch. "Ten minutes."

"I've been doing this for half a day."

"It's been two minutes, Grandpa."

Tough soldier face. Sucked in his gut, kept going; picked up the hand weights on the table.

Tree wished there were exercises to help you get strong after your parents got divorced.

He and his brothers could use them.

Larry was hardly ever home—when he was home, he'd just lie on the couch, watching TV.

Curtis didn't seem to want to do much.

They hadn't gone to a movie yet.

Hadn't practiced basketball together.

Tree wondered if divorce was like war and always had a lasting effect on the people who went through it.

CHAPTER EIGHT

Sophie Santack was standing at the popular-eighth-grade-girls' table in the Eleanor Roosevelt Middle School cafeteria, determined to make a point. She looked smack into the beautiful face of Amber Melloncroft.

"I'm not here to make trouble. I just want to know how come, ever since I showed up at this school, you look at me like I fell off a garbage truck."

A gasp rose from the popular girls assembled as Amber, their leader, looked at all of them like she *couldn't* believe this. . . .

Sophie gripped her tray. "I just want to get one thing clear. You're not any better than me. I'm not crawling with bugs or have green slime running down my neck. I'm a person just like you."

Amber made a shocked noise of disgust and all the other girls made the exact same noise.

"I've moved around a lot. What's at this school isn't all that different from other places. We don't have to be friends, but we don't have to be enemies, either."

And with that she walked off and sat at the back of the lunchroom by herself.

It was near the table where Tree sat with Sully Devo and Eli Slovik—far away from Jeremy Liggins, who used to "accidentally" spill chocolate milk on Tree.

Sophie was looking at her lunch and, it seemed to Tree, trying not to cry. A mean laugh rose from the popular-girls' table, followed by whispers, giggles, and stares at Sophie. Tree hated it when girls did that. He thought Sophie had been brave. Tree knew that Amber would get back at Sophie every chance she got. Sophie had started at the school a few months ago and didn't have any friends.

Tree knew what that was like. Sometimes it felt like every seat in the world was saved for somebody else.

He looked at Sophie and said something he'd never said to a girl. "You want to sit with us?"

Sully and Eli looked shocked because, first of all, they were seventh-graders, and a seventh-grade boy never sat with an eighth-grade girl. And second of all, Sophie was weird.

Sophie shook her head.

"We're not crawling with bugs or have purple slime running down our necks." Tree surprised himself by saying this.

Sophie half smiled. "It was green, the slime I mentioned."

"Slovik's got green slime on his neck, but he's done eating." Eli punched Tree in the arm. "So, you want to eat with us?"

"Okay, well . . ."

They only had seven minutes before the bell rang, but in that time Sophie told them close to her whole life story.

"Okay, so the last place I lived was in the Bronx—we were there for three years—and then my aunt Peach and my mother decided it was cheaper to live here, so we moved, and we're all living in an apartment, which is torture, over by the railroad station—me, my mom, my cousin, my aunt, six cats, and my iguana, Lassie. There should be a law that makes trains be quiet so people can get their sleep. When I'm a lawyer—if that's what I do—I'm either going to be a lawyer or have my own talk show. I haven't decided. But, one way or the other, I'm going to take care of problems. We don't know what the future's going to bring, but I figure law and talk aren't going away. And I was just born with a big mouth—my aunt Peach tells me that all the time—so I guess I'm going to use it. They named me Sophia because it stands for wisdom. I usually say what people are thinking and don't have the guts to say." She took a bite of her sandwich. "This is the worst food of any school I've ever been at. We should do something about this. Demand justice. People have more power in this world than they think."

Tree had never heard anyone talk like this.

Sully and Eli hadn't, either.

"Okay." Sophie was moving her head back and forth in a kind of rocking motion, like she was listening to music that only she could hear. "So, here's how it is. Here's my motto: Speak your mind and ride a fast horse. There's just one problem."

"You don't have a fast horse," Tree guessed.

"You got it. What's your name?"

"Tree. That's what they call me."

"What's your motto?"

Tree thought about that. "I don't have one."

"You've gotta have a motto."

Tree looked at Sully and Eli. They didn't have mottoes, either.

"How do you know what you're about?" Sophie slurped down the last of her milk.

Tree, Sully, and Eli weren't sure how to answer.

That's when the bell rang.

Sully and Eli got up gratefully.

Tree said to Sophie, "I'll think about it . . . the motto thing. . . ."

"Dad, do you have a motto?" Tree had been thinking about this most of the afternoon.

"Well . . ." Dad looked at the coffee mug he was holding from his store: *Kramer's Sports Mart: We Will Not Be Undersold.* "I've got a slogan, does that count?"

"Not really."

Curtis and Larry weren't home to ask.

Grandpa said, "I always liked what the POWs held to. Return with honor."

"That's good, Grandpa."

Tree went into his room, sat at his desk, took out paper and a pen. Wrote the mottoes he knew.

Speak softly and carry a big stick.

The buck stops here.

You can't teach an old dog new tricks—Tree knew that was a lie; he wasn't sure if it was a motto.

Do unto others as you would have them do unto you.

That was a decent thought, but it didn't sound cool like *Speak your mind and ride a fast horse.*

Tree tried to edit the words, make them better.

Finally he came up with *Treat people the way you want to be treated.*

He wondered if that was good enough to be a motto.

He looked at the *Tyrannosaurus rex* model on his desk. He'd put it together with Grandpa when kids were teasing him about his size in fifth grade. Tree related to dinosaurs, but wasn't too thrilled about the extinction part.

"They died off because they were too big," Jeremy Liggins would taunt him. "They died because they were slow and stupid and they needed too much food."

Tree remembered gluing all the teeth into place, how Grandpa sanded the pieces of the tail when Tree told him what Jeremy had said.

"So, how do you want to be treated?" Grandpa asked.

"Just like I'm regular. Like I'm not so big."

"The problem is, you're not a regular size. How do we work around that?"

Tree didn't know. He just wanted to be regular.

"How about wanting them to treat you with respect, even though your size makes you stand out?"

Tree nodded.

"How are we going to get them to do that?"

"I don't know."

"I think the only way it can happen is if you try to treat them with respect first." Grandpa fastened the last tail part on with glue, held it down with his thumb.

That wasn't the easy answer Tree was looking for.

"You've got to just think of yourself as a farmer laying down seeds. There might be some storms and weeds that choke what you're trying to grow. But you'll get a crop eventually. I guarantee it."

Tree looked at his motto sheet, underlined *Treat people the way you want to be treated.*

He wondered if dinosaurs had mottoes.

Probably *Eat your enemies before they eat you.*

"So, I guess people say a lot of stupid things to you about your height."

Sophie said this to Tree in the hall when he was slurping deep from the drinking fountain. He was so surprised, he half choked. She threw down her flute case and punched him on the back.

"Breathe, or I call 911."

Tree waved her off, coughing.

"You know why people do that?"

Tree coughed. "Do what?"

"Say stupid things."

"I'm not sure."

"My aunt Peach says they say them because they don't know better, and if they do, it makes them feel like they've got one up on you."

Tree hadn't thought of it that way.

"So, what do they say?" Sophie was looking up at him.

"They say, 'How's the weather up there?'"

"That's dumb. What do you say?"

"Usually nothing."

"Spit on them. Say, 'It's raining.' "

Tree laughed. "They ask me if I take a lot of vitamins."

Sophie was shaking her head.

"They ask if my parents are tall, what size my shoes are."

She looked at his substantial feet. "What size are they?"

"Sixteen double E."

"So, you've got a presence. You show up, people notice."

Tree smiled. "I guess so." He liked thinking about it that way.

"There are worse things." She picked up her case. "I've been playing the flute since I was eight. I'm close to being a musical genius except for when I've been blowing for an hour and my mouth gets full of spit."

That's when Laurie Fuller and Char Wellman, two popular eighth-grade girls, walked up to Sophie, snickering.

"So, did you?" Char asked Sophie, and she and Laurie giggled.

"Did I what?" Sophie held her case tight.

"Fall off a garbage truck?" Laurie asked, and they both exploded in laughter. "Is that how you got here?"

Sophie looked right at them. Tree felt his whole body go stiff.

"I got here in a Chevy," she said quietly.

The girls ran off, triumphant. The dirty deed done.

Tree stood there, shocked.

"I gotta go," Sophie whispered.

And she went.

CHAPTER NINE

Tree stood in the same place in the hall by the drinking fountain for so long, it seemed like he'd grown roots. He was thinking of all the things he could have said to defend Sophie, but none of them were any good.

He remembered how Jeremy Liggins once said that Tree was "a giant freak that shouldn't have been born." Tree knew this wasn't so. He knew his parents and grandpa loved him. But some words and the way people say them are like grenades exploding on a battlefield.

"Never try to outrun a grenade," said Grandpa. "Just leap away from it, hit the ground, and pray you're far enough away."

VA Rehab, 0800 hours (8:00 A.M., military time).

Grandpa came here three times a week to work with Mona.

"I'm just a little concerned, Leo, with you playing Santa Claus this year."

The Trash King, one of Grandpa's best friends, said it. He

ran a trash pickup business. They'd served together in Vietnam. He'd driven Leo and Tree here in his truck.

Grandpa cranked hard on the arm machine. He'd been Santa Claus every year at the children's hospital when the Vietnam Vets Association did their annual show.

"Kids are going to want to crawl on your lap, Leo. You handled it last year, but I knew you were hurting."

"Santa Claus knows no pain." Grandpa said it tough; a stab of pain hit his leg.

King studied his old, stubborn friend. "You could branch out. Be an elf."

"I don't want to be an elf."

"You could be a reindeer."

"Mona," said Grandpa, "I've kicked butt on this machine. Give me something harder."

She laughed. "Take a break, Leo."

"Why?"

"Because you're making me tired."

Tree laughed, helped Grandpa get off the machine. He didn't need as much help as last week.

Of all his grandpa's Vietnam buddies, Tree liked the Trash King best. He worked for him sometimes, moving old, busted furniture like couches, lamps, and tables. King would sell them to "people who had vision."

"You give me a person with vision," he'd say, "they can take the most broken-down piece of junk and turn it into something beautiful. They don't let a few scratches worry them. They see to the heart of the piece."

Tree pushed the wheelchair in place. Grandpa plopped down, chuckled. "Santa Claus in a wheelchair could start a new trend."

"You could get hurt, Leo."

"Mona," Grandpa shouted, "tell this man what disabled people can do."

Mona Arnold folded her arms, shouted back, "Just about anything."

Luger, who'd gotten decent at holding a cup, grabbed it with his mechanical hand and raised it high.

King knew when he was outnumbered. "All right, Leo. You're on deck. But the elves are watching. If you can't handle it, they're moving in like Green Berets."

"Men . . ."

Coach Glummer walked slowly before the Pit Bulls. "I've been given a revelation that will have a lasting effect on this team."

The Pit Bulls looked concerned.

"Basketball is like a dance, men. We need to find the rhythm of the game, flow more as a team. Move from side to side like you're dancing."

Tree had never danced. Most of the Pit Bulls hadn't.

"Like you're dancing with a girl, you know. Going across the dance floor."

Tree didn't know. He'd never danced with a girl.

He tried to picture the basketball like a girl, but no girl he knew would appreciate being dribbled.

"Try some flowing movements." Coach Glummer began to sway back and forth.

Tree moved an inch.

"Throw your body into it."

Tree didn't want to do that with his body.

"Ballroom dancing," Coach Glummer announced. "It'll teach you balance, how to move across the floor with a partner, how to trust your body, and ultimately"—he looked at the basketball net—"how to win on this home court and beyond."

The Pit Bulls turned to stone.

"My cousin Sheila is starting a class at the Y. Tuesday nights from seven to nine. Maybe you got the flier."

All the Pit Bulls had gotten the flier. They had thrown them into the garbage in a great show of team unity.

"I want you to sign up. That's an order. You'll thank me for this in the weeks and years to come."

He blew his whistle. They were dismissed. But they all stood there desperately trying to think of why Tuesday nights couldn't work.

"I take allergy shots on Tuesday and, you know, Coach, I can puff up," said Petey Lawler.

"Tuesday nights I've got to watch my little sister," Ryan Trout pleaded.

Colin Renquist had the best line. "Dancing makes me puke."

The Fighting Pit Bulls exploded in laughter.

Coach Glummer was unmoved. "Bring a bucket, Renquist."

■   ■   ■

Tree's father had been carrying a bucket since he got home from work, sure he was coming down with the stomach flu. Sure he was going to start heaving any moment.

Tree was worried about him. "Is there anything I can do to make Christmas easier, Dad?"

He put the bucket down, looked monumentally sad. "We're just going to get through it."

Tree had hoped for more than that.

Dad touched Tree's shoulder. "I'll be okay, buddy. I've just got to work things out."

"I think Mom made a big mistake when she left." Tree had never said that out loud before.

Dad leaned against the wall. "It wasn't just her, Tree. I could have done a lot of things better. I could have tried to understand her more. I wasn't too good at that."

"Do you think you guys could . . . maybe . . . decide this isn't a good idea?"

Dad half smiled. "Your mom thinks the divorce is a good idea."

Tree looked down.

"It takes time," Dad said, "to get used to all this."

How much time, Tree wondered.

It was midnight. The sounds of handball echoed in the basement.

Thump.

Thwack.

Tree hadn't heard those sounds in a long time. His dad had

61

been a handball champion back when he lived in New Jersey. But he was too busy to play these days; too tired.

Tree headed to the basement to watch.

Thump.

Dad hurled the little handball against the basement wall; stepped back to cup it in his right hand as it bounced toward him. The best thing about this house was the high basement ceiling.

Thwack.

The wall had ball marks on it. The marks had always bothered Tree's mother, who wanted to paint the wall yellow.

Handball walls are gray.

Any guy knows that.

Thump. Thwack.

There's a rhythm to handball.

Tree sat at the top of the basement stairs and watched. It seemed to Tree that his dad was always happier when he was moving. Tree was happiest when he was taking things apart.

It's funny how life gets so complicated, you don't get to do the thing that makes you happy. You have to concentrate on the things that are expected.

His dad should have been a coach.

Run a sports camp for kids.

Thump.

His dad had helped Curtis and Larry all through school athletics. He'd tried to help Tree, too, especially in football.

"Size-wise, Big Man, you've got the potential to be one mean defensive lineman."

"I don't know, Dad."

"Just crouch down and hold your arms out. There's no finesse required."

If Tree could have changed one thing about himself, it would have been that he was better at sports and shared that with his father.

He looked at the glass case on the other side of the basement. Curtis's and Larry's sports awards were there: most valuable player certificates, athlete of the year trophies, Larry's medal for most home runs in a season.

Tree had never once won an award.

The little handball spun off the wall. Dad made a low catch. Gently threw the ball on the wall with English. Looked up, saw Tree watching him. Did his famous triple ball bounce off two walls and caught it behind his back.

That move used to drive Tree's mother bonkers. She'd run to the basement door and shout, "Is everyone all right?"

Funny the things you miss when you don't have them around anymore.

Dad threw the ball easy to Tree, who missed the catch.

It bounced off the stairs and rolled beneath the washing machine, where handballs go to die.

"Sorry, Dad."

Now the thunder of older brothers racing down the basement stairs. Older brothers who were good at handball. First-string.

"Come on," Dad said to Tree.

"I'll just watch." He didn't want to look stupid.

Dad served. Larry caught it low, spun it on the wall. Curtis caught it between his legs, returned the bounce strong.

Thump.

Pow.

Thwack.

Larry went all out for every ball; grunted, groaned.

Curtis had more confidence, but Larry played harder.

Larry could lie on a couch for hours looking half dead, but put a ball in his hand and he'd catch fire.

They were having so much fun.

They wouldn't, probably, if Tree joined in. He always felt he slowed things down.

He felt like a woolly mammoth in a world of tigers and antelopes.

A giant sloth moving slowly up a tree when all the squirrels and monkeys had gotten there first.

He sat at the top of the stairs like he'd done most of his life.

He acted like he didn't mind.

But he did.

CHAPTER TEN

"Choose how you'd die," Sully said. "Shark attack, alien abduction, or"—he shuddered—*"ballroom dancing."*

It was the first night of ballroom dance class. Sully, Eli, and Tree were standing behind the big bush near the entrance to the Y. From the front, Sully and Eli couldn't be seen; Tree poked out like a giraffe in a necktie.

"Not dancing," said Eli, who'd offered his parents half of his $123 life savings if he didn't have to take this class.

"Maybe an alien," Tree said.

Sully loosened his tie; his mother had yanked it tight like a noose. "I'd take the shark. But I'd need to have a heart attack first."

Cars were pulling up to the entrance. Girls in dresses got out excitedly. Boys in badly fitting suits slumped in misery toward the front door.

"It could be worse," Sully said. "We could be dead."

"We could all just not go," Eli suggested. "Who'd know?"

"Okay," said a familiar, tough voice from behind. "You guys

going in or what? 'Cause the sooner we get started, the sooner it's going to be over. Those were Aunt Peach's parting words to me."

Tree turned around, and there was Sophie looking very pretty in a purple dress, her hair done up in a barrette, and her black eyes flashing total attitude, which is exactly what you'd want in a dance partner.

Coach Glummer's cousin Sheila looked at the eighty-seven seventh- and eighth-graders assembled in the gym of the YMCA. Her teacher's heart fluttered with care for her students. She wanted to become a trusted person in their lives, a teacher not just of the fox trot, the waltz, and the tango, but a role model of enduring memory.

But Sheila knew that eighty-seven seventh- and eighth-graders could turn on her at any moment. So she stood on center court and shouted, "I'm the law in this room. That means what I say goes. If you disobey, you're out, and I keep your parents' money. *Do we understand each other?*"

Eighty-seven heads nodded grimly.

"Ballroom dancing can be one of the most fun things you'll ever do. For that to happen, you have to listen like your life depended on it. Are you still with me?"

They were.

"We begin dancing like we begin most new things—by taking a risk. I'm going to demonstrate a simple step that will get you through most wedding receptions. This is as easy as life gets. Watch. *Right foot forward, left foot matches, right moves back and left detaches.* You try."

The Fighting Pit Bulls looked at one another glumly. Tree glanced over at Sophie, who was looking at the ceiling.

"Right foot forward, left foot matches. Right moves back and left detaches."

No one got it right.

They moved into dance circles. Sheila's Romanian dance partner, Lazar, who swayed constantly even when there wasn't music playing, worked with the boys.

"Okay now, young mens." Lazar tossed his head, swaying. "I'm gonna teach you how, you know, to go with it."

Lazar did a few slow steps. "You see from that? You see to just move and go with it? Okay, mens, let's slide."

The Pit Bulls were particularly bad at sliding.

The evening went downhill. Sully and Eli were sticking their fingers down their throats, pretending to vomit.

"We're going to put some of these steps together."

Partner time. The popular boys raced for Amber and her friends.

Sully said he was sick.

Eli said he had to get a bucket for Sully.

Tree hoped that dancing with someone would be better than dancing alone.

He walked slowly up to Sophie, who was studying the floor.

Cleared his throat.

Waited.

She looked up. *"Well?"*

"I'm here," Tree said.

"And?"

"I was going to ask you to, you know . . ." He looked around. "Dance."

"You need to say the words. Would you like to dance?"

"I would," Tree said.

"*No*—you ask *me*."

"Right. Would you . . . like to dance?"

She took his hand, smiled bright. "I'd be delighted—and I'm not just saying that."

They walked onto the middle of the floor. Tree was absolutely the tallest person in the room. Lazar and Coach Glummer's cousin Sheila locked into position, which seemed easier for shorter people.

"Good posture," shouted Sheila. "If you get lost, just watch me and Lazar."

Tree bent down to reach Sophie's waist. Her head came up to his chest. He took her hand gently; didn't want to squish it. He wasn't sure his left foot could detach at this angle.

He could either dance or have good posture—not both.

Sophie laughed. She had a good laugh. Solid, not tinkling. "You look like you're at a funeral."

"I'm sorry."

"Aunt Peach dragged me here by my nose hairs, but it's not as bad as I thought."

Tree nodded.

Dumb music started playing.

Tree took the deepest breath of his life and forgot everything he'd been practicing for the last ninety minutes. Sophie was right there with him, messing up.

Tree had no idea how this would help him in basketball or in years to come. But it sure was nice to be so close to Sophie.

"It's weird here now, huh?"

Tree took his tie off and said it to Curtis, who was lying on the couch at Dad's with an empty pizza carton over his face.

"I mean, with Mom and Dad and everything. . . ."

"It's weird," Curtis agreed, not moving the carton.

Tree flopped into the chair.

"I'm here *all* the time." Tree wanted to make this point. He felt like a soldier that had been fighting a battle on his own, just waiting for fresh troops to come in and give him a hand. "Sometimes I'm not sure what to think."

"I'm not, either." Curtis took the carton off his face, looked inside, ate the last bit of cheese. "We went to Mom's house tonight. Me and Larry. Larry called it Munchkinland."

Tree nodded.

"We helped her trim the tree." Curtis sighed. "She told the ornament stories. This one we got on that Christmas farm in Iowa. This one we got in Bermuda."

He didn't mention it was like being at a funeral, remembering the dead.

Didn't tell Tree the next part, either.

How Mom kept asking them, *"Are you all right?"*

What do you say?

"No," Curtis had said finally. "I'm not. I'll be all right. But this is hard, Mom."

"Why did you buy this house?" Larry asked her.

"It was the only one I could afford!"

"Why did you get this dog?" Larry wouldn't let up.

"Because I wanted company! You're blaming me for this divorce, and that's not fair!"

Tree took his shoes off, studied his big toe sticking out of his sock. Looked at Curtis. "Why do you think they got divorced?"

Curtis crushed the pizza carton. He wanted to get back to school, where things seemed normal. Tree looked kind of pitiful to him. As the oldest, he'd seen and heard more of the fights. The ones about his father's job were always loud.

"Why," Mom would shout at Dad, "are you content just running a sporting goods store? You have so many gifts that you've never developed."

"I *like* sports."

"That's not an explanation."

"Not everything in life has to have an explanation!"

And she would storm off saying that *she* wasn't going to just settle for whatever came. *She* was going to improve herself.

"Go for it," Dad would yell.

The next morning, they would be in the kitchen with faces like cement.

Curtis sighed. "I don't know how it happened. They just changed. They stopped doing things together that they used to do. They stopped laughing. They began to have really different lives. Dad worked mostly; Mom worked, went to school, and rearranged the furniture."

Tree half laughed. "Remember that time Dad came home

and sat where his brown chair had always been, and fell down and started shouting?"

"I thought he was going to punch a hole in the wall."

"And then I'd meet him at the door when he came home and tell him if Mom had changed stuff around while he was gone."

Curtis nodded. "You were always good at things like that."

They looked at the scrunched-up pizza box.

"Do you think," Tree asked, "they'll change their minds? I mean, if Dad learned to understand her more, they could get back together maybe. It's not like they hate each other."

"I don't know, Tree Man. I don't think so."

"I wish they'd waited till I was in college."

Curtis smiled. "They might have killed each other by then."

"Do you know the secret to fighting a war?"

Grandpa asked Tree the question as they were folding the laundry. Grandpa always dove deep doing laundry.

Tree didn't know.

"You've got to hold on to the things you know to be true, set your mind to a higher place, and fight like a dog to keep it there. War can be so fierce, you can forget the good. Forget what you're about in this world, what's really important. There's always going to be somebody who wants to try to make you forget it. Don't let them."

Tree wasn't sure how you do that in seventh grade.

He folded a towel and remembered the day his mom moved out.

August twelfth, a bright, sunny day. A day where you wouldn't think anything bad could happen. He'd just come back from helping her move. There in the dryer was a full load of her clothes she'd forgotten to take. He gathered the clothes in his arms, started up the basement steps, couldn't handle it. He dropped the pile and ran into his bedroom, crying.

A knock on Tree's bedroom door.

He was madly drying his face with his sleeve. Grandpa came in.

"You okay?"

"Yeah."

"Convince me."

Tree told him about the clothes.

"I would have cried, too, if I'd seen that." He limped over— his leg was so bad—sat on the bed. "It's the things we don't expect that just rip the scab off."

"She was supposed to pack everything."

"She meant to. It's been a hard day. People do all kinds of things they wouldn't normally do when they're fighting each other. I'll help you fold that laundry, then you call her, let her know it's here."

Tree walked to the basement steps, gathered up the clothes.

His mother had used fabric softener. Her yellow robe was soft and smelled nice. He half buried his nose in it like Bradley snuggled his old towel.

He lugged the laundry to his room. He and Grandpa folded each piece like it had cost a fortune. Tree called Mom at her new house, and she started crying. She'd come over and get it, she said. She hadn't meant to leave it.

Tree hoped he wouldn't think about this every time he did the laundry.

"It's tough around here now, I know." Grandpa held up five unmatched socks, looked in the hamper for the others. "We've all lost a piece of ourselves. War does that—it blows things up and leaves an empty place where something important used to be."

"Is that how you feel about your leg, Grandpa?"

"Yep. Is that how you feel about your mom and dad?"

Tree looked down. "Kind of."

"I'll tell you something about empty places. They don't get filled in right away. You've got to look at them straight on, see what's still standing. Concentrate on what you've got as much as you can."

Grandpa dug around the hamper, couldn't find the missing socks. He started laughing. "I don't need a pair of socks. I just need one. Doing the laundry gets easier when you're not so particular."

Tree laughed, too.

You've got to love a man who can teach you to laugh at war.

CHAPTER ELEVEN

"Okay, Aunt Peach, so this is my friend Tree."

Tree was standing in the hallway of Sophie's apartment. It was cramped and dark.

Piles of laundry all around.

Lassie, the iguana, in a cage on the dining room table.

Cats on the couch; cats in the hall.

Aunt Peach was chasing one of the cats that had just clawed the drapes.

She stopped, gazed up at Tree, way up. "You're a big one."

Tree slouched a little.

Aunt Peach ran off. *"Dimples, I'm going to break your furry neck!"*

Tree and Sophie were going to take the bus to the Midas Muffler shop in Baltimore where her dad worked. She was going to give him her Christmas present.

She knew he wouldn't have anything for her.

"He's not so good at presents," Sophie said.

"He's not so good at life," her mother added from behind the bathroom door. "Don't expect much, Sophia."

Sophie put on her coat, tucked a little wrapped present in her backpack. "I expect the bus'll get us there, Ma. I expect it'll be cold outside. That's it."

A flush. "Don't take the wrong bus."

"I've done this before."

Running water. "Don't stay long."

"He gets a fifteen-minute break."

Bathroom door opened. Sophie's mother stared up at Tree. She looked just like Sophie except for being older and rounder. "If he asks about me, tell him I'm dating three movie stars."

Sophie laughed.

"You deserve a better father."

"But he's the one I got." Sophie pushed Tree out the door.

The Midas Muffler shop was packed with people drinking coffee from Styrofoam cups and checking their watches. Sophie pointed to a big man with his head inside a car engine.

"That's him. The big guy. You've got something in common already."

Sophie's father seemed satisfied with what he'd done; he motioned for another man, who got in the car and drove it out. He walked toward the glass door—didn't smile, didn't frown—pushed it open.

Sophie got nervous, her hands went in every direction. "Okay, Dad, so this is my friend Tree."

Sophie's father looked at Tree. "How old are you?"

"Twelve."

A snort. "You think I'm stupid?"

"No, sir. I'm really tall for my age."

"You're tall for *my* age." He stepped closer. *"You know how old she is?"*

"Dad—"

"No, really." Tree grabbed his wallet, got his seventh-grade ID. He had a copy of his birth certificate, too. His mother made him carry it.

Sophie stepped in. "Okay, so we know you're busy, Dad, and we don't want to mess up your schedule here."

Sophie's father studied the ID, handed it back.

"I brought you a present, Dad, on account of it's Christmas soon." She handed it to him.

"I left yours at home." He always said that. He lit a cigarette, blew smoke rings out slow.

"I recorded some Christmas music for you on my flute. I got your favorites. 'God Rest Ye Merry, Gentlemen' and 'Jingle Bells.' " She's talking faster, too fast. "I call it *Sophie's Greatest Christmas Hits.* The last half of 'O Little Town of Bethlehem' got cut off 'cause my cheeks were getting exhausted from all the blowing."

"I'll play it in the car."

"I hope you like it."

"You still got that flute, huh?"

"Yeah. I practice a lot."

He put the cigarette in his mouth, gave her a good pat on the shoulder.

"Vinnie!" Another man shouted it. "You on vacation or what?"

He looked at Sophie, softer this time. "I gotta go."

"Sure," she said quietly.

"Hey, Soph, we'll get together."

"Anytime, Dad."

He patted her shoulder again. Shook Tree's hand. He had a killer handshake.

"Size matters, kid. Wear it proud." He pushed through the glass door.

Tree stood straight.

Sophie's mother was right.

She deserved a better father.

"He can take a muffler out faster than any man alive," Sophie said. "They had a contest here last year and he won by three whole minutes."

"It was nice, what you gave him." Tree didn't know what else to say. He couldn't imagine having a father like that.

"I'm glad you think so, because it's the exact same thing you're getting for Christmas."

"My dad doesn't know how to love people," Sophie explained. "He drove my mother crazy."

The bus was late. They stood there shivering.

Tree clapped his hands together to stay warm. "I guess my parents drove each other crazy, too."

Sophie marched in place so her feet wouldn't freeze. "I got sent to a therapist about it. She told me I had hidden anger at my father and it was coming out when I was with other people. I told her no way was there any anger hiding in me. 'Open your eyes,' I said. 'It's all here on the surface.' But I figure I've got it better than a lot of kids. At least I know where my dad is."

Tree had never once thought of that.

The bus pulled up. She climbed inside.

"You coming or what?"

Tree got in the bus, hit his head.

She laughed. "You need a bus with a sunroof so you can stick your head out."

Tree didn't think that was funny.

Sophie elbowed him. "You've gotta laugh. If you don't, you'll cry."

CHAPTER TWELVE

Getting Grandpa in the Santa suit reminded Tree of the time when his mother had bought an outfit for Bradley—a sweater, hat, and booties—and Tree had to put it on him.

"Standing's not an ability I've got right now!" Grandpa tried to steady himself as Tree tried to pull the big red pants over his legs.

"It would help," Tree said, "if you'd stop moving so much."

"It would help if I had two working legs."

"Let's go with what we've got, Grandpa!"

Finally the pants were on. Grandpa looked at the floppy pant hanging loose over his half leg.

The Trash King adjusted his elf cap, cigar in his mouth. "You could say a reindeer chewed it off." King put on his pointy elf shoes, struck a pose. "Am I hot or what?"

"Scorching," said Grandpa. "But lose the cigar."

"It's not lit."

"You've got to be a role model."

King put the cigar in his pocket. "And you've got to be

careful, Leo. We tell the kids you've got to save your strength for Christmas Eve, when an angel's gonna come down from heaven, touch you with a magic wand, and your leg's gonna grow back."

Grandpa looked in the mirror Tree was holding up, put rouge on his cheeks, fastened the big white beard. "We're going to ruin this holiday for hundreds of children."

King picked a cigar leaf from his teeth.

"Ho, ho, ho," said Tree halfheartedly, folded the wheel-chair, and carried it to the truck.

"The thing about Christmas," the Trash King said, driving his truck to the children's hospital, "is how I didn't understand what it was about until I got to Vietnam. You remember Christmas in Nam, Leo?"

Grandpa sighed. "I was in the hospital."

"That's right. You didn't get to see the show." King turned the corner. "They brought in a big show from the States with singers and dancers. There were hundreds of us out there watching. A couple guys had made a Christmas tree out of bamboo and painted it green. I was feeling sorry for myself because I wasn't home.

"And then we started singing. Just singing the songs. 'Silent Night,' 'Jingle Bells,' 'We Wish You a Merry Christmas,' 'Hark, Those Herald Angels Sing.' And I could have sworn—and a few guys in the Signal Corps would back me up on this—that there was a star in the sky a little brighter over where we were. And I thought, We get these holidays all wrong. We think it's what we get and how we feel and how warm and cozy we are, but Christmas came to all us slobs that night and most of those guys weren't expecting it. Some of us hadn't even washed. Now, I'll tell you how this helps me in trash. . . ."

King pulled up to the hospital parking lot. Grandpa groaned. "Save it, King, for the ride home. We've got a job to do."

Tree got the wheelchair from the back, placed a red throw blanket over it. Carefully eased Grandpa out of the truck and into the chair.

"Santa has landed," said King.

"You bet your boots, Elf Man."

Grandpa adjusted his beard, waved them forward like a lieutenant leading a platoon into battle. "Let's take this hill."

He grabbed the chair's wheels with his strong arms and pushed through the emergency doors that swung open at the miraculous power of Christmas.

"Ho, ho, ho," Grandpa bellowed to young and old who looked up excitedly.

"The Big Guy's here!" the Trash King shouted. "We're going to party tonight!"

Tree laughed and waved and shook all the hands of all the kids who came up to him. Down the hall they went with the ho-ho-hos booming. Kids in wheelchairs were following them. Tree handed out candy canes; King had a bag of toys over his shoulder. They turned the corner, saw three vets dressed like reindeer. Luger marched forward dressed like a toy drummer, beating a snare drum with his good hand.

Rat tat tat.

Rat tat tat.

Rat a tat. Rat a tat.

Tat tat.

A doctor took them into the rooms of the children who were too sick to come out.

One little girl had an IV in her arm and looked gray. Her mother was sitting in a chair by her bed. When Grandpa rolled in, that child lit up like a Christmas star.

"Santa," she whispered.

"You've got it, kid."

"You're in a wheelchair."

"Life isn't perfect, is it?"

King pulled a stuffed bear out of his bag, gave it to her. She hugged it, smiled at Tree.

"Santa, would you tell me a story?"

"Sure."

"Would you tell me 'The Night Before Christmas'?"

"Sure. Where's the book?"

She looked concerned. "Don't you know it?"

Grandpa looked at Tree and they both looked at the Trash King, who sniffed and said, "He knows it."

Grandpa desperately tried to remember the poem. The little girl hugged her bear and smiled.

"Okay, here goes. . . . 'Twas the night before Christmas, and all through the house, not a creature was stirring, not even a mouse." He stopped dead.

"The stockings," the little girl said.

"Were hung by the chimney with care," said King.

Grandpa grinned. "In hopes that Saint Nicholas soon would be there."

Silence.

Tree whispered about the kerchief, the cap, and the nap.

They got through it, helped by the little girl and her mother, and they had to call in two nurses to get the names of the eight reindeer right. King insisted the front reindeer were Dasher, Dancer, Prancer, and Nixon.

"Vixen," shouted the older nurse.

"Jeez. They named a reindeer *that?*"

They didn't miss a room that night.

Didn't miss a child.

Dozens of children lined up to see Santa. First in line, a boy in a big leg brace. He looked at Grandpa's half leg. "What happened to you?"

"I had an operation."

"Does it hurt?"

"Sometimes."

"Mine hurts, too. I wouldn't want anyone to sit on it."

So he stood next to the wheelchair and told Santa how he wanted a complete model train set, *not* like the one he got last year, like the one *Billy Buckley got* with the cool engine and the miles and miles of track.

Grandpa motioned to King. "Take that down."

"I didn't bring any paper."

"Elves," said Santa, shaking his head.

They had a party in the cafeteria for the kids who could get there; everyone sang Christmas songs. Only a few stalwart believers sat on Santa's knee, and he managed. Then a little girl climbed up on Tree's knee and told him that she wanted her lung to get better for Christmas.

Tree didn't know what to say.

Then she whispered, "I know you can't really give me that. I just wanted to tell you."

And she hugged him like he was the genuine article.

It made Tree feel about a foot taller, which was really saying something.

CHAPTER THIRTEEN

Tree didn't need much more of Christmas to happen after that.

Except it would have been nice if Larry stopped yelling at Bradley, who, according to Larry, wasn't moving fast enough to get out of his way.

"Take it out on somebody your own size!" Tree shouted.

"Like you?" Larry shouted back.

Tree stood tough. "I'm bigger than you!"

Larry's face darkened. "Maybe I could do something about that!"

But he never did. Larry was a screamer, not a fighter.

Twice he'd come home at night really late. His voice sounded different, he swayed when he walked. Grandpa said he'd been drinking. Larry got grounded, but he snuck out again anyway. When Larry staggered into the house at 2:00 A.M. with beer on his breath, Grandpa said, "What you're doing isn't making the hurt go away."

Larry stood there, quiet.

"Booze doesn't help. Talking does. Time. And I'll do whatever I can to—"

Larry shouted at him to mind his own business.

Grandpa said that anything that had to do with Larry *was* his business.

Larry raced up the stairs, flopped onto his bed. A few minutes later, Bradley pushed the door open and stuck his old snout on Larry's arm.

"Get lost!"

But Bradley wouldn't. He just sat there with his big trusting eyes waiting to help. Finally Larry hugged Bradley around the neck, buried his head in that good, old fur, and cried his eyes out about his parents' divorce.

Right after that, he sank to his knees in front of the toilet and vomited up beer until his insides felt raw.

Eight P.M., December 24.

Tree, Curtis, Larry, and Grandpa looked at the half-bare living room.

Tree hadn't realized how important Christmas trees were until he didn't have one.

Larry said, "Some Christmas."

Curtis said, "Shut up."

They'd been at each other all day.

Grandpa grabbed his walker, struggled up. "We're going to change things here. We're going to form a squad—tough and unified. And don't tell me it can't happen. I saw it happen in Nam. Saw different people with nothing in common work together to a common goal and become strong friends. So strong, you'd do just about anything to make sure your buddies stayed alive."

He rolled the walker to the middle of the living room. "That's what it comes down to sometimes—forgetting how you feel; being brave in front of your friends."

Curtis, Larry, and Tree were quiet.

Bradley, who understood about friendship, trotted in from the hall.

"We need a Christmas tree," Larry said finally.

Grandpa nodded. "That would help."

"We could get one at the store," Tree suggested.

"The stores," Curtis snapped, "are *closed.*"

Grandpa grinned. "Guess we'll have to steal one."

In the car.

Curtis driving too fast, yelling at Tree to scrunch down in the backseat.

"You try scrunching down back here!"

Curtis screeched into the parking lot of Kramer's Sports Mart. Dad was just about to close the store down. Curtis stopped fast. Tree's head hit against the driver's seat.

Wheelchair out. Too many arms to help Grandpa.

"Wait," said Larry, "I lost my grip."

"Dear God . . ." said Grandpa, sliding butt to the door.

Wheeling toward the store. Tree ran ahead, opened the doors.

Their father at the cash register, trying to clear out for the holiday. He looked up, shocked.

"This is a stickup," Grandpa boomed cheerily. "Just hand over the tree and nobody gets hurt."

"What?"

Grandpa pointed to the Christmas tree in the middle of the store, complete with lights and ornaments.

"You're closing. You don't need the tree. We do."

"Pop, it's not my tree. It's the store's tree."

"You're the manager." Grandpa motioned to the boys, who started unplugging the tree, arguing about the best way to get it out.

"I need it back on the twenty-sixth when we open."

Grandpa looked around. "We'll take that wreath and that fake holly."

Tree got the wreath. Larry got the holly.

"Pop . . ."

Grandpa wheeled himself toward the door.

"It's Christmas, Bucko, we're going to start acting like it."

Tree lay across the seat with the tree placed over his body. Sports ornaments dangled in his face.

"Drive carefully," Grandpa ordered Curtis, "or he'll be scarred for life."

Tree groaned all the way home to make the point.

They got the tree up.

It filled the empty spaces of the living room.

Dinner cooking. Dad and Grandpa in the kitchen, getting in each other's way.

Huge steaks. A dozen fat tomatoes. Three loaves of bread.

Four tins of pound cake. Frozen strawberries. Endless cans of whipped cream.

Bradley looked longingly at the tree.

"Don't even think about it!" Curtis gave Bradley a push out the door.

Then Dad remembered he left his presents for everyone at the store, and Tree remembered he left his presents for everyone at Mom's house, and Curtis and Larry remembered that they should have gone shopping, but didn't. And Grandpa said they didn't need presents, they just needed to let Christmas come natural, like the first one.

Bradley started barking at the front door. Tree let him in. Bradley headed right over to the Christmas tree, lifted his leg, and peed and peed.

"See," said Grandpa, "if we had presents under there, they'd be ruined."

And Bradley slept soundly in the hall.

CHAPTER FOURTEEN

"Pommerantz!" shouted Mom. "Don't eat that. *Bad dog!*"

She ripped a celery curl with chutney cream cheese from Pommerantz's tiny teeth.

Aunt Carla, Mom's sister, came over to defend him. She and her dog were visiting from Florida for the holidays.

"He's not a bad dog, Jan. He just doesn't understand. Do you, Pommie?"

This was almost more than Tree and his brothers could stand.

Conan started barking. His territory had been invaded.

You learn the flexibility of the human spirit when you have two different Christmas experiences in less than twenty-four hours.

"How's your . . . father?" Mom asked in that edgy way.

"Okay," Tree, Larry, and Curtis said together.

"Grandpa?"

Same response.

She looked at the Serenity Fountain, a gift she had given to herself. Gentle, gurgling water cascaded over small, peaceful rocks. This is what her life would become. Someday.

She was trying now to be conversational with her sons. "How was your Christmas Eve?"

"Pretty good after we stole the tree," Curtis offered.

"What?"

Tree hit Curtis in the arm, told her the story, tried to make it light. He left out how he had to lie underneath the tree in the car.

"Your dad loves to do things last-minute."

She looked at her decorated kitchen with the little wreaths of basil over the sink, the Christmas music playing softly, the three kinds of vegetables, the perfect pies. Last night she had finished decorating the house with garlands, pinecones, and blue and white bows.

She'd strung popcorn, for crying out loud.

She'd pictured everyone smiling and happy, but instead her sons seemed distant and sad. "Let's talk about our feelings."

"That's a good idea," Carla chirped.

Three distinct male groans.

Mom wiped away a tear. "We all know it's different this Christmas. We're still in the fresh pain of the divorce, the awkward parts of how to be with each other." She looked at her sons. "Don't you think?"

Tree nodded.

Curtis and Larry didn't commit.

"We can make this work if we talk. If we don't talk, we'll never know what's going on." She grabbed the supersize bottle of Motrin she kept by the sink, gobbled three pills, looked at the gurgling Serenity Fountain. "You can tell me anything, and I promise I will listen. I love you guys more than I know how to say. There is no wall between us, and there never will be. I want to know all that's happening in your lives."

Three pairs of shuffling male feet. Larry looked up finally.

"I'm kind of flunking two courses, Mom."

Apron flung off, gums back like Conan. *"What are you saying to me?"*

"You wanted to know what was happening!"

"You'll lose your scholarship!"

"I can't concentrate. I don't know."

"Flunking? Not even a D?"

"Yeah! I get up every morning and say, 'How can I really screw up today?' "

Larry stormed out of the room.

Carla said, "He's acting out his feelings of frustration and anger, Jan."

Mom turned in fury to Tree and Curtis.

Curtis had overdrawn his checking account again, but he was taking that news to his grave.

Tree thought about mentioning how he'd taken apart the blender a couple of weeks ago and there were two parts missing and he wasn't sure it worked, but his mother was standing in front of it now with a handful of walnut halves—she put them inside the blender and everything in Tree wanted to shout, *Don't.*

She flipped on CHOP.

Nothing.

She checked the plug, tried again. The blender made a sound like a sick duck. Dark fury came over her face. She turned to Tree.

Tree was famous for doing this.

He took the answering machine apart when his mother was looking for work.

He took the remote control apart when his father's commercial was running during the Army-Navy game.

"You will *never* do this again."

Tree gulped. "I promise."

"I think a fire in that pretty new fireplace would be nice," said Carla, running from the room.

Mom furiously chopping the walnuts by hand.

Then concern hit her face.

"Was the flue up or down?"

"I think we've got a problem here!" Carla's voice was an octave higher.

"No!" screamed Mom.

They all ran into the newly painted living room and watched as billows of black smoke blew into the room while the logs crackled in the fireplace.

"Guess it wasn't open," said Curtis.

Tree grabbed a broom from the closet, knelt down by the fireplace, breathing smoke, coughing as his lungs filled with it. He shoved the broomstick up to where the flue should be. Shoved four times, finally felt it pop open.

"Open the windows!" Mom screamed. *"Open the door! Open everything!"*

Larry ran down the stairs. "What happened?"

"Doom," Curtis said solemnly.

"Oh, God, Jan, I'm so sorry!" Carla was opening windows, batting smoke from the air.

Pommerantz was barking pitifully in the kitchen.

"Oh, poor Pommie. He must be so scared."

Pommerantz ran into the hall, stood shaking on the little yellow-and-white hooked rug, and puked up the celery stick with cream cheese.

"Pommerantz," screamed Mom, *"sit on a tack!"*

"I think that's excessive, Jan."

It was then that the smoke alarm in the kitchen went off.

Mom stood on a stool by the freshly baked pies, trying to turn it off; the siren blared.

She yanked it from the freshly painted ceiling.

Ripped out the batteries.

And finally, quiet came upon them.

Except for the gurgling drips from the Serenity Fountain.

Mom crumpled on the floor in a woeful heap. The aroma of perfect roast beef wafted from the oven.

"Smoke alarm works," said Curtis, who was known for having a firm grasp of the obvious.

Tree, Curtis, and Larry half laughed from relief.

She didn't think that was funny.

Tree scrunched down next to her, put his arm around her shoulder. "You've got to laugh, Mom. If you don't, you'll cry."

CHAPTER FIFTEEN

"My little sister is allergic to Fred."

Eli Slovik told Tree this on the phone. Fred was his parrot.

"She's got some feather allergy and Fred has to be out of the house until they test her and see if there's medication. Can I bring him to your house? Just for a little bit?"

Tree wasn't sure how Bradley would handle a parrot.

He wasn't sure how anybody would.

"He could keep your grandfather company, Tree. Just ask. *Please?*"

"Back off, Buster."

Fred the parrot said it to Grandpa, who said, "Back off yourself. I'm going to teach you some manners."

Bradley looked at the parrot and barked loud.

"I really appreciate this, Mr. Benton." Eli was holding the big cage with Fred inside. "He gets kind of excited sometimes."

Grandpa stared at Fred, who stared back.

"I've got to go, Mr. Benton. Thanks." Eli looked in the cage. "You be good, Fred."

"Back off, Buster."

Eli looked pained. "My uncle taught him to say that."

Bradley backed out of the room.

"You're certainly looking handsome today, Leo." Grandpa had his walker close to Fred's cage. "Go ahead, bird, say it."

Fred looked back.

They were getting used to each other.

Grandpa tried again. "You're certainly looking handsome today, Leo."

Nothing from the bird.

"That'll get you a whole lot farther in the world than 'Back off, Buster.' "

"Back off, Buster," Fred announced.

Grandpa sighed, headed back to the couch.

The white oak stood like a skeleton covered with snow. It was hard to look at it and remember how full and lush it had been in the spring, how its leaves had turned to wine in the fall. That's the thing about winter—it's so easy to forget the other seasons—it never seems like it will end.

Tree stood in front of the leafless white oak. He could see every branch, all the textures of the gray bark.

Tree wanted it to be spring, but dealt with the reality.

He picked up an acorn. It was so small, so compact—the seed of a new tree just waiting to be released in the earth.

With his boot, he dug a little hole in the cold ground, put the acorn in it, covered it with dirt and snow.

He liked the idea of planting a new tree.

He thought about his grandpa's new prosthetic leg, which was going to be coming soon. Mona Arnold said Grandpa was going to have to learn to walk a whole new way and it wasn't going to be easy.

They'd gotten through Christmas.

Curtis and Larry were back at college.

It was January now.

And Tree still hated his mother's house and the teeny rooms, he still hated the frozenness he felt sometimes as the fresh divorce kept coming at him in the strangest ways.

Like at night, when he would suddenly get a bad stomachache and feel scared for no reason.

Like at Eli's house, when he felt so sad when Eli's dad kissed Eli's mother.

Like at school, when Sophie told him she'd call him as soon as she got home. She said *home* like it was permanent condition.

"Where are you this week?" she asked.

The every-other-week color-coded schedule had started again.

"My mom's."

"You've gotta stop saying it that way. You've got two houses. There are worse things." Sophie mentioned living with six cats who all had their own kitty-litter beds.

"I think the stress is getting to Lassie. She's not crawling on her branch as much. She used to go crazy when I'd play 'The Ash Grove' on my flute, but now it's just another song. I'm getting worried."

Bradley was getting slower, too.

Tree tried drawing pictures of happy dogs running and jumping, but Bradley just looked at the pictures, sighed, and took a nap.

He was napping a lot these days.

Then Bradley started pooping on the hall rug.

Tree would clean the mess up as best as he could. But Bradley kept having accidents.

"We're going to have to do something about this, Tree," his dad said. "Bradley's getting old, too old maybe to have a decent, productive life."

Tree's whole body went cold. He remembered when Sully had his dog put down.

"I'm a good guy," Dad added. "I try to give everybody a break, but Grandpa can't get around the way he used to and you're only here every other week."

"I'll teach him to do better, Dad, *I swear.*"

Tree was on his knees, patting the back half of Bradley. Patting as much life into him as he could.

Dad grabbed his pounding head. Went to the basement to do his laundry. He'd been recycling dirty socks all week.

Tree cleaned up the mess.

"Bradley, this is serious."

Tree took paper, drew a rug with dog turds on it, put an X through it, held it up.

"This rug is a no-poop zone."

Bradley listened intently.

"You poop outside." Tree drew a porch with steps and the

big evergreen in the front lawn with a pile of turds under it. *"Got it?"*

Bradley cocked his head. He liked being talked to.

Tree wasn't a great artist, but he could get an idea across.

Tree was in his ski jacket, sitting on the front steps with Bradley. He looked at his old dog—half sleeping, breathing deep.

A squirrel scurried by. Not so long ago, Bradley would have chased it.

"It would help if you chased something, especially when Dad's watching." Tree drew a so-so squirrel being chased by a dog. Held it up. "It looks like a mouse, but it's a squirrel."

He had showed Dr. Billings, the veterinarian, his method, but the vet said dogs don't learn that way.

Dr. Billings was a good vet, but not too creative.

The front door opened.

Dad stood on the cold porch. "What I said about Bradley . . . I know that scared you. I'm sorry."

A loud car honk sounded. Bradley didn't move. He used to bark when those things happened.

"We just have to figure out what's best for him."

Tree nodded.

McAllister, Mrs. Clitter's ugly cat, was slinking across the lawn.

Bradley opened one eye.

He didn't like McAllister. No one did, except Mrs. Clitter.

McAllister crept closer.

Closer.

Too close.

The old dog barked, rose to his feet.

Tore after McAllister.

Bradley trotted back when McAllister was off the property. Lay back down on the porch.

Tree's father shook his head, laughing.

"*Yes!*" Tree shouted.

There was life in that old dog yet.

CHAPTER SIXTEEN

"Awright, Pit Bulls!" Coach Glummer shouted from the side-lines. *"Let's come alive out there!"* He clapped his hands. *"Let's see some mad-dog hustle!"*

But it's hard to find energy and hustle when the scoreboard reads

VIKINGS 43

PIT BULLS 4

That score stood stark like a tree without leaves.

Halftime. Coach Glummer clinging to hope.

"Forget the first half. Forget that all but two of you played like sheep. The past is gone!"

The Pit Bulls weren't sure what that meant.

"Think of yourselves as blank sheets of paper, and write on that paper a winner's story!"

In the bleachers, Tree's dad leaned forward.

"That huge kid's a joke." A father sitting a row back said it to another father. "All that height, not a clue how to use it."

Furious, Tree's dad stood up, applauding. *"Let's go out there!"*

Back on the court. Tree tried to think of himself as a winner.

Not missing a shot.

Awesome in power.

I am a tree.

He stepped in front of an average-size Viking, held his huge arms out. Snarled briefly.

The Viking looked for a way to pass the ball, but this is hard to do when a tree is in front of you.

The ball dropped.

Tree grabbed it. Felt a sureness as he dribbled down the court.

Tree's dad cheering him on.

Coach Glummer shrieked, *"Give me the slam dunk of a winner!"*

Tree aimed.

Missed.

Jeremy Liggins got the ball on a rebound.

Made the basket.

"Now, that kid's got the moves," the father a row back said.

Just one basket, Dad thought. *Let him get one lousy basket.*

Liggins made six more points before the game was over.

Tree never scored.

But somehow, Tree felt pretty good.

Almost like a winner.

But you know how it is with coaches.

They want the win, not the concept.

"I'm sick of most of you guys not trying," Coach Glummer snarled in the locker room. Looked at Tree when he said it.

Tree got so angry at that.

Jeremy Liggins sauntered up to Tree: "You're a joke out there."

But something in Tree rose up.

"No, I'm not." He squared his shoulders and looked down at Liggins, who looked away first.

February brought bad weather.

The temperature shot up and the rains came with a fury.

February brought more business travel for Tree's mom. She had less time at home, which meant Tree only stayed with her a few days every other week.

He was glad to spend the extra time with Bradley and Grandpa.

He checked heymom.com every day, though.

Clicked on *What We're About* to read reminiscences of him and his brothers growing up.

Clicked on *The Road Ahead* for at-a-glance thoughts on how divorced families heal and grow *(Trust + Time = Tenderness)*.

He never clicked on *Just Between Us* or *Hugs*.

The computer can take you just so far with your mother.

But one kid's snack is another kid's dinner.

He showed Sophie the website. She scrolled down the page, amazed.

"Your mother does all this for you? You don't know how good you've got it."

■   ■   ■

"You're a genius."

Bradley cocked his head as Grandpa looked at Fred the parrot, who looked back.

"You're a genius. Say it, Fred. Come on."

Grandpa had given up on Fred ever saying, "You're certainly looking handsome today, Leo." Tree's dad suggested that Grandpa could call Mrs. Clitter, and she'd come over and say he was handsome.

He needed the bird's respect.

"You're a genius," Grandpa tried again. "Say it, Fred. Make me glad you're here."

Fred ruffled his emerald feathers and squawked.

The rain kept coming.

Grandpa was looking toward May and the Memorial Day parade. His new leg was supposed to be delivered any day now, but it got held up because of the weather.

"Where's my leg?" he kept asking Mona.

"It's somewhere in Chicago, Leo."

"What's it doing there?"

"The plane it was on had to land because of the snow."

"I've got to be marching strong by May."

"Leo, I can't promise you'll be marching anywhere by May. It takes *time* to get this right."

He held up his hand, didn't want to hear it.

"I want you to push me hard, Mona."

"I'm not going to push you any harder than makes sense."

The next day:

"What's my leg doing in Miami, Mona?"

Grandpa half shouted it on the phone.

"United Airlines put it on the wrong plane, Leo, and now they're not sure where it is in the airport."

"Maybe we should send in the paratroopers to get it back. I'm going to be a genius at this walking business, and my leg is seeing the country."

CHAPTER SEVENTEEN

"Leo," said Mona Arnold, grinning, "meet your new leg."

She handed him a flesh-colored leg cut off below the knee.

Grandpa held it. "Look at this miracle, will you?" He felt the weight. "It's heavier than I expected."

"Once you get used to it, it takes your weight and gives you a nice fluid movement."

Grandpa studied it.

"If you just sit down over here, Bill will show you the next part."

Bill, the leg man, brought out the stump sock, the liner sock, showed Grandpa how to put them on. He fitted the leg on the stump, showed how the mechanism clicked tight.

Tree and his father were there to meet the new member of the family.

Grandpa worked for two hours, practicing.

Standing on the leg.

Taking it off.

Walking so carefully a few steps, a few more.

Tiring, focused work.

Every step counts. Every step teaches something.

"Swing your leg out more, Leo. That gives you an even step."

"Try to put equal weight on both legs now. This'll take some time since the good one has been taking so much of the weight."

"If you go too far too soon, you're going to get redness and swelling. Easy does it. This isn't a race."

He sat down, took the leg off, held it in his lap.

"You can put it on the floor," Mona said.

"No way. We're bonding."

"Vietnam wasn't our war. That's what the bigwigs in Washington told us."

Grandpa had been thinking about that the last few days. Every so often he'd take the war apart to try to make sense of the experience.

He was sticking his leg on, practicing walking in the house with Tree.

A couple of faltering steps.

The first steps of the day are the hardest.

"There we were on the battlefield, getting shot at, dying, but it wasn't our war. That was so confusing." He looked at Tree. "You ever feel like that?"

Tree wasn't sure. "Sometimes I feel I'm in the middle of Mom and Dad's divorce. They're fighting each other—not me—but I'm there."

"You learn to duck. That's what I did."

Tree laughed. "I know about ducking."

Three more steps.

Step, drag the leg. Step . . .

Grandpa gripped a chair for balance. "I ran for cover a lot, too. And I tried to remember the things I had control over so I wouldn't feel like a grunt."

"Like what?"

"Like how I responded to people. How I kept my weapon clean and ready. How I always wore my helmet. I protected my head come hell or high water. Guys would kid me about it." He laughed. "Figures I'd get shot in the leg."

Grandpa stood in front of the full-length mirror in the hall. Looking in mirrors helped him see if he was standing right.

He straightened up a little, smiled at Tree.

"I think you and I have a lot in common. We're both learning to walk a different way, and we're both going to be geniuses at it."

More than anything, Tree wanted to be like his grandpa.

Grandpa shouted to Fred the parrot in the living room, "You're a genius. *Say it, bird.*"

"Back off, Buster."

Grandpa shook his head. "You think I can walk a few blocks in this thing next week? I've got something I need to do."

"Put them down there."

Grandpa handed Tree a new deck of playing cards in a plastic bag. Tree put it near a wreath of flowers and a baby picture that were soaked from the pouring rain.

Grandpa reached up to touch a name on the Vietnam Veterans Memorial in Washington, D.C.

Private Elmo P. Hothrider.

Grandpa and Tree had driven here with the Trash King.

"Elmo was a fine card player. He got shot up bad outside Da Nang. His eyes were bandaged shut when I went to see him in the hospital. And you know what he wanted? He wanted to play cards. So I played for him and me. Elmo won three hands out of five, and he accused me of cheating."

Grandpa touched the name again. "Rest well, friend. Don't take any wild cards up there."

He limped to another section of the wall that stretched long and black across the mall in Washington, D.C.—an hour's drive from Ripley.

"That's the place."

Tree put a bottle of hot sauce near Sergeant Nick Marconi's name.

Candles, flowers, family pictures, a big bottle of Hershey's Syrup. Anything can hold a memory.

He placed a letter in a plastic bag and put it on the wet ground for Corporal Michael Diggins. Grandpa stood by Corporal Diggins's name for a long time as the cold rain beat down.

"Diggins always said the jungle was crazy. You think you're going the right way, but you're really going back the way you came. It changes color with the sun and the clouds. You're waiting to fight, and you start thinking the shadows are going to come get you. Then you realize that war is as much about your mind as anything else. Is what you're seeing real, or is it made up?"

The Trash King reached up, touched Calvin Merker's name. Merker dragged six injured people to safety before he was shot himself.

King stood there like he was waiting for something.

Tree had heard enough about the war to know that a big part of it was about waiting. Soldiers waiting for their marching orders, pilots waiting to fly their missions. Everyone waiting for it to be over.

"So many," Grandpa said, limping from end to end as rain poured down.

Tree tried to imagine what some of these soldiers looked like; he never could. He didn't know if they were tall or short, fat or thin. A name on a wall didn't tell you that. But Tree knew that all the names here and the people who came to remember them were connected with a special kind of courage.

Grandpa alongside him now, struggling on that new leg. "Every friend I lost, I still carry in my heart. The paratroopers do it right. They put out an empty boot when one of them dies—no one can fill that shoe.

"We hear about casualties on the news—114 dead. Two murdered. Over three thousand killed. Numbers don't tell the story. You can't measure the loss of a human life. It's all the things a person was, all their dreams, all the people who loved them, all they hoped to be and could give back to the world. A million moments in a life cut short because of war."

CHAPTER EIGHTEEN

Tree wished there was a memorial wall for divorce.

If there was one, he knew what he'd leave in tribute.

The photo of his parents laughing on the beach.

He kept it in his sock drawer, but that didn't cut it as a memorial.

"More rain expected today, folks."

That's what the weatherman said on TV. Tree was at his mom's house.

"Thunderstorms continue throughout the week." Weather laughter. "It's not my fault, I swear." The northeast section of the weather map showed storm clouds, lightning flashes, and blinking raindrops.

"They started sandbagging the levee in Burnstown." Mom said it, sipping coffee. Burnstown was three towns away. "Don't be late for the bus."

Tree got his slicker, bent down so Mom could kiss him on the cheek.

"Stay safe out there, sweetie."

Conan yipped.

And Tree headed out into the cold, wet world.

The bus was late again.

Tree stood waiting for it in his iridescent slicker, pummeled by wetness. He felt like some giant glow-in-the-dark road marker.

Other kids were waiting, too.

No one spoke.

Endless bad weather makes you not care much about anything.

Sully, who'd lost two raincoats last week, showed up completely covered by Hefty bags. He stood morosely next to Tree.

"Can you see?" Tree asked him.

"No."

"You want me to make your eyeholes bigger?"

"No."

The bus pulled up, splashed water on their legs, sloshed it in their shoes. Thunder boomed.

Tree helped Sully onto the bus.

From inside the Hefty bags, Sully spoke.

"Close the school. We're too wet to learn." He raised a bag-wrapped fist.

Students nodded.

The bus lurched through the storm.

Outside the middle school orchestra room, Sophie was unwrapping ten layers of plastic bags from around her flute.

"Aunt Peach says if the flute gets ruined, I don't get another one. I told her it would be a real loss to the music world. I've got this big tryout and I've got to play dry. I want this solo bad, Tree."

Flute sounds came from the orchestra room.

"That's pretty," Tree said.

"*That's* Sarah Kravetz playing." Sarah Kravetz was Amber Melloncroft's best friend. "She wants the solo, too. She can't even hit a high C."

Tree listened some more. "She's not as good as I thought."

The flute music stopped.

"I get mucus in my throat when I'm nervous." Sophie cleared her throat like a truck driver, spat into a tissue.

"You'll do great," Tree offered.

Sarah Kravetz walked out, looked Sophie up and down like she'd fallen off a garbage truck. Didn't even look at Tree.

Flounced off.

"So, okay, I'm next."

Sophie cleared her throat loud as Sarah looked back, amused; Amber joined her, whispering.

Sophie on her knees, searching through her book bag for the music.

"I had it this morning."

Giggles.

Tree wanted to punch a hole through the wall and shove them in.

"Okay. Wait." Sophie held Poldini's "Dancing Doll" high so Amber and Sarah could see.

And with that, Sophie Santack cleared her throat, spat big,

113

and marched into the orchestra room to show what a tough kid could do with a tender instrument.

I GOT IT!!!!!!!!!!!!!!!!!!!!!!!!!!

That's what Sophie's note said on Tree's locker.

He looked for her in school. Walked though the packed halls, towering over the heads of students, but he couldn't find her.

Sully lumbered by on his way to the principal's office, sent there for turning his hearing aid off in social studies.

"Haven't seen her," he said glumly.

I GOT IT!!!!!!!!!!!!!!!!!!!!!!!!

She held up a sign when he was at basketball practice.

Tree grinned at her, focused on the net, and actually made a basket.

He tried to act like he did that all the time, but inside he was soaring.

Sophie stomped on the bleachers.

"I got it!" she said excitedly when he came out of the locker room. "I got the solo at assembly *and* I got the solo at the Memorial Day concert after the parade. I'm going to be a soldier of yesteryear and play this medley of war songs I've never heard before, but I'm going to know them in my sleep by May. It's going to be a lot of pressure, but I think I'm up to it. Mr. Cloud said I had true feeling for the instrument."

Tree beamed. "That's great."

"And I needed this, Tree, 'cause people don't always get

where I'm coming from. Those eighth-grade girls don't get it."

"I know."

"I'm going to bake brownies and bring them to school tomorrow. We're going to *celebrate*."

Chapter Nineteen

She smelled it before she saw it.

Couldn't figure out what the awful odor was.

She turned the corner, holding the plate of brownies.

She'd fixed her hair extra nice, too, with that purple barrette.

Sophie was feeling as good as she'd ever allow herself to feel.

But then she saw it.

Trash bags with smelly garbage hanging from her school locker, piled around the floor, spilling the stinking mess everywhere.

Tuna cans.

Coffee grinds.

Broken eggshells.

She dropped the brownies.

Tore the barrette out of her hair.

Stood there frozen. Kids walked past her, holding their noses at the smell.

"I didn't do this, okay? I didn't bring this here!"

Then she saw the sign—in pink block letters.

GARBAGE GIRL

She tore it down just as Tree ran up.

"Who did this?" he shouted. But he already knew. "We'll clean it up. Sully, Eli, and me. You won't have to—"

Teachers were coming now.

Students saying it was awful.

The bell rang.

They stood there.

Mr. Cosgrove pushed a Dumpster into place; moved quickly. Took down the bags, threw out the garbage.

"They're going to explode someday from all the garbage inside them," he told Sophie, but it didn't make her feel better.

She grabbed a smelly tuna can and stormed off.

"Sophie," Tree shouted.

She kept walking.

Tree ran after her. "Where are you going?"

"I've got someone to see." She was almost running, holding that can.

Pushed into first-period geometry—her class—stormed right up to Amber Melloncroft and Sarah Kravetz, who looked away, trying not to smile.

Mr. Pelling, the math teacher, said, "You can't walk in here like that."

Sophie slammed the can down on Amber's desk.

"If you and your friends ever do that to me again, you're going to be sorry!"

Amber shouted, "I don't know what you're talking about, and take your lunch off my desk!"

Sophie picked up the can, shoved it under Amber's up-turned nose. "This is a smell you know real well."

"That's enough!" Mr. Pelling shouted.

"She's threatening me!" Amber wailed.

"No." Tree stood tall. "She's telling the truth about what you did. Now everybody knows." He stepped closer. "I want to know *why* you did it."

"Get away from me, you overgrown freak!"

"What made you think you had the *right?*"

"In the hall!" Mr. Pelling pointed at Tree and Sophie.

He marched them to the principal's office.

"Threatening a student," he told Mrs. Pierce, the administrative assistant.

The principal was on the phone with the superintendent.

They had to wait.

"Dr. Terry," Tree said to the principal, "Sophie didn't threaten anybody. Those girls have been mean to her for a long time."

Dr. Terry leaned back in her chair. "Several teachers told me what happened with the locker. It was an awful thing to do. I apologize to you, Sophie, on behalf of this school. That is not what we're about. But you should have come in here to talk to me as soon as it happened."

"I never think about principals when I'm mad."

Dr. Terry smiled. "I understand."

"I don't know if you do, Dr. Terry. You didn't see it."

"Sophie, something like this takes time to fix. I'm going to talk to Amber and her friends. I'm going to talk to their parents and to this school community at large. There is zero tolerance for cruelty at Eleanor Roosevelt. I'll call your parents, too, so we can work this out together."

Sophie looked down. "I don't think I want to come back to this school."

Tree's heart just broke for her.

Dr. Terry leaned forward. "I'm asking you to give me a little time to make this right."

"I'm in eighth grade, Dr. Terry. Unless I flunk, you haven't got much time."

Aunt Peach arrived at the school, folded her considerable arms, and eyed Sophie like a prison guard.

"What are we going to do about your temper?"

"They put garbage on my locker, Aunt Peach!"

"That was a cold, cruel thing to do."

"And I let them know it. Sometimes you've got to shout the truth and wake people up."

"Sophie, I like to think that truth doesn't need to be shoved down people's throats."

"In eighth grade, Aunt Peach, truth needs all the help it can get."

CHAPTER TWENTY

"I told Aunt Peach I'd rather eat dirt for a week than come to ballroom dancing, but she said it's going to help me socially." Sophie folded her arms tight. "Like there's hope."

Sophie stood miserably in a red dress near the wall of the YMCA gym, as far away from Amber Melloncroft and Sarah Kravetz as possible.

Tree stood next to her.

Sully and Eli were out front, hiding in the bushes.

Coach Glummer's cousin Sheila tossed her head; Lazar tossed his.

They stood cheek to cheek, arms extended, knees bent.

"The tango," Sheila said, "is making a comeback, and I want you to experience it."

They rotated dramatically, not smiling. Lazar bent Sheila back.

"The tango is about *passion*."

The boys started laughing, especially Jeremy Liggins. The girls giggled.

"The tango is about despair and emotional power. It was born during a time of great economic hardship. People danced it to express the sadness in their hearts."

Sophie looked at Tree, who knew he wasn't up to this.

"Don't be afraid of passion and despair," Sheila shouted. "We all have deep rivers running through us. This dance will help you find them."

"I'm there." Sophie grabbed Tree's hand and marched onto the dance floor.

After sixty minutes of tango practice, Tree had found despair.

He was too tall for this dance.

To look directly into Sophie's eyes, he had to bend low.

To fully extend his arms with Sophie's, she had to grab his elbow instead of his hand.

He almost dropped Sophie when he had to lean her back.

And the worst part was, Sophie loved it.

"Okay, we're going to connect to our deep rivers of despair, Tree, and get so sad, we can hardly stand it. We're going to let all the garbage that's been thrown at us come out and show these people what's what."

Tree was absolutely certain he couldn't do that.

But Lazar picked Tree and Sophie and Amber and Jeremy to demonstrate.

They walked to the middle of the dance floor.

Amber looked at Sophie, held her nose.

"Mr. Cosgrove should have put *you* in the Dumpster," Sophie snarled.

"You are *so* pathetic!"

"You think so?"

Tree stood tall, stared at Amber. "Stop it!"

Amber looked away.

Silence from Jeremy.

"Together with the eyes," Lazar shouted.

Sophie's dark eyes fixated on Tree.

"Okay. From that, young peoples, we find our sadness!"

Hands on hips, Sophie stepped defiantly past Amber, who was having trouble finding anything. Sophie tossed her head, posed with pain.

A big part of the tango is posing.

She did a little twirl around Tree, who almost went in the right direction.

He stood there like a stage prop, trying to keep his deep rivers to himself.

Sophie stomped her foot, her red skirt flared up. She glared at Amber, who looked down.

"You see from that?" Lazar shouted. "The girl, she becomes the dance."

Painful music swelled.

And Sophie Santack owned that dance floor.

She didn't really need a partner, but Tree wasn't giving up his slot. She came close: "We're going to try that cheek-to-cheek thing and pray to God we don't mess up."

Tree prayed.

Bent down to reach her cheek.

"Stand tall," Sophie told him. "Wear it proud."

They danced cheek to chest, which was a whole lot easier.
Tree bent her back for the finish.
The music ended.
But not the pain.
That's the point of the tango.

CHAPTER TWENTY-ONE

The only thing the continuous rain was good for was Eli's little sister, Rachel, whose feather allergies got better, and the doctor said Fred could come home.

Grandpa had complicated feelings about this.

He hadn't once gotten the parrot to say he was a genius.

"Back off, Buster" was all he got. That bird was stuck like an old record.

He'd hoped to bring Fred to a new level of communication, but it wasn't meant to be.

"I would like us to begin a new level of communication."

Tree's mother said this on the speakerphone in her kitchen to Tree's father, who was at work.

Tree was in his mother's living room, listening.

Mom scrolled down her computer screen. She'd typed out exactly what she wanted to say.

"I think we're strong enough to do this now, Mark. I know it will be important for the children."

Silence. She geared up for the next line:

"I know that we are forever linked to each other because of the kids. We need to be able to talk together and make decisions together without all the old stuff getting in the way."

Tree's father didn't say anything because his stockperson had just dropped a box of golf balls and the balls were rolling everywhere.

"Are you still there?" she asked.

"Yes." Dad stopped a golf ball with his foot.

"Did you hear me?"

"I heard you."

"It would be nice if you at least acknowledged you heard me."

"I heard you." Dad stopped three balls with a hockey stick. He didn't like talking about important things on the phone.

Mom lived on the phone. *"Well?"*

This, thought Tree, is the old stuff.

Mom and Dad decided to talk about it next week at dinner. At Dad's house, so she could say hello to Grandpa.

They said good-bye in that edgy way.

Tree wondered if they would ever talk to each other easily again.

He walked into the kitchen.

Tree wasn't sure he should confess. But he did.

"I kind of overheard, Mom."

"Your dad and I don't want to let our problems stand in the way of doing the best for you and your brothers."

Tree nodded. That was nice.

"I'm not going to let years of misunderstanding stand in the way of being a forgiving adult."

She wasn't done.

"Your dad and I shared important moments. I'm not going to let them get buried." She said that pretty fast.

"It's good you can talk," Tree offered.

She turned off her computer, sighed. "It's going to be hard for me to go to the old house."

"I know, Mom."

"I haven't seen Grandpa and Bradley for . . ."

"They miss you. We all do."

Her eyes teared up. "I'm crying so much these days. I'm sorry. I see a baby and I cry. I see a kitten and I can hardly stand it. I see a commercial with a happy family eating vegetables and I fall apart."

"Maybe we should stop eating vegetables," Tree offered hopefully, handing her a box of tissues.

She blew her nose. "Should I bake something for next week? Anything you'd like?"

Tree laughed. "You should probably bring the whole dinner, Mom."

Twisting the tissue. "Your dad said he'd take care of dinner. I don't want to insult him."

"Your mother's coming for dinner."

Tree's father said this at six o'clock.

Tree was shocked. "I thought she was coming on Thursday."

"We changed it." Dad checked his watch. "She'll be here in thirty minutes."

Tree looked around—no food on the stove, in the oven. "What are we eating?"

"I don't know." Tree's father wrung his hands.

"Sophie's coming over, Dad. Remember? We're going to watch that TV show on lizards since her TV's broken. You said it was okay."

"It's okay." Already Dad regretted this whole evening.

"But *Mom's* coming."

"That's okay, too."

He picked up the phone to order pizza.

For men, there's always a simple solution to dinner.

"Well . . ."

Mom sat at the dining room table, looked at the empty walls, the shadows of where the hutch had been.

Remembered how they'd fought about who got the hutch.

Studied the clothesline and pulley system on the ceiling. Felt a tightness in her chest.

"It was an experiment, Mom."

"I'm sure it was."

She smiled at Tree, looked kindly to Grandpa, patted Bradley's old, loyal head. Bradley hadn't left her side since she'd walked through the door.

"We haven't sat at this table together for a long time," Mom said quietly.

Dad moved a can of motor oil off the table to make room for the pizza.

"Sausage or veggie?" he asked too loudly.

Mom's smile grew thin. "I don't eat sausage. I never have."

"Right." Dad cut into the veggie pizza, slapped a huge piece on a paper plate, looked at his ex-wife. "We've got salad."

"Please."

Salad plopped on the plate. Too much dressing.

Lightning cracked in the sky; the hanging light over the table flickered just like in a horror movie.

Mom turned sympathetically to Grandpa. "How are you, Leo?"

"Sausage or veggie?" Dad asked Grandpa.

"Whatever's easy."

Dad froze. He needed facts.

"Give him one of each, Dad." Tree said this miserably. "I want sausage. No salad."

"You should have salad," Mom said.

"I'm not hungry, Mom."

"Give him some salad."

A teaspoon of salad dropped onto Tree's plate.

Dad made a pizza sandwich—slapped two pieces of sausage pizza together facedown; took a huge bite.

Mom looked away. She hated it when he did that.

Grandpa asked, "How's it been going for you, Jan?"

She picked at her salad. "I'm traveling a lot. Teaching more seminars. We've been streamlining the curriculum. I have to do a three-day workshop in a day and a half now. I'm not sure everyone is learning what they need. It's frustrating. Not as frustrating as what you're dealing with, Leo."

"I handle it. I'm walking in the mall. You know how much I love shopping."

She laughed. "I didn't think anything could get you in the mall."

"Only raw courage, rehab, and rain, Jan."

She laughed. "Leo, I haven't been by to see you because . . . well—"

He held up his hand. "It's been a tough time. I'm just glad to see you now."

She took his hand.

The doorbell rang.

"I think that's my friend."

Tree went to the door, opened it to Sophie, who stood there, drenched, holding something big and square covered in a plastic bag.

A car horn. Shouting voice: "Two hours, Sophia. That's it."

"Okay, Ma."

Tree waved at the car. Rain poured down.

"I brought Lassie. I wanted her to see this."

"Boy, that's real nice you guys can have dinner together without killing each other."

Sophie stood by the table, holding Lassie's cage. "We've had a lot of divorces at my house. My aunt Peach got a restraining order against her second husband. If he comes closer than thirty feet from her, she'll have him arrested. She carries one of those snap-up rulers to keep things legal. We don't mess around in my family."

Mom stared at the cage, not a lizard lover.

"This is Lassie, my iguana. I named her that 'cause I'm

working up to a dog. I wanted Aunt Peach to get used to the idea. She's pretty upset these days."

"Your aunt Peach is upset?" Mom asked.

"Lassie's upset." Sophie shoved the cage in Mom's face. "See how she's not moving much? She used to have a good personality. Her head would go up and down when I talked to her. I think the weather's got her depressed."

Booming thunder in the distance.

"The weather's doing that to all of us." Mom pushed her chair back, wondering where this young woman came from.

"Your show's probably on," Dad said weakly.

Sophie checked her watch, sat at the table, put Lassie in front of her. "We've got a couple minutes. I just wanted to say that you guys do this divorce thing right. When my parents split up my mother said, 'Your father's a moron. I'm kicking him out.' "

Tree stood fast, grabbed Lassie's cage, and headed for the television.

The doorbell rang.

Tree got the door, holding the cage.

It was Mrs. Clitter holding a basket.

"Now, how is that man—"

She stopped dead, stared at Lassie.

"It's an iguana," Tree said.

"But she's under a lot of stress," Sophie explained from behind. "She's missing other lizards, so I brought her over here."

Mrs. Clitter looked confused. "There are other lizards over here?"

"There's a nature show on lizards starting. I'm going to let her watch it. The vet says iguanas are exotic animals and won't examine her for less than seventy-five dollars. My aunt Peach says hell's gotta freeze solid before she gives a vet that much money to take an iguana's pulse."

"I baked bread," Mrs. Clitter half shouted. "Have I come at a bad time?"

Grandpa kept his mouth shut on that one.

Mrs. Clitter sat at the table and joined the party.

The lizard on the screen was creeping up a tree limb, bobbing its head.

"See, Lassie, that could be your sister," Sophie said.

Lassie was sitting on her rock, watching Bradley instead of the TV lizard.

The doorbell rang.

Mom got up, opened the front door.

The Trash King stood there holding a salami. He grinned. "Are you kids back together?"

"We're *just* having dinner."

Dad closed his eyes.

"Well, you never know what these things can lead to, Jan. Just be open to the world of second chances." He winked. "That's what keeps me in business."

He walked into the dining room. "Leo, I brought a salami."

"And I brought bread," said Mrs. Clitter.

"Okay," Sophie shouted from the next room. "Lassie's doing the dance."

Lassie was bobbing her head like the TV lizard.

"She just needed a role model. She needed to know she wasn't the only lizard in the world."

Sophie's bobbing now, too.

The Trash King got out his Swiss army knife, cut hunks of salami, handed them around.

From the dining room he could see Sophie bobbing. "Do the dance, Lassie. Do it."

"Who's that kid?"

"That's what we're all wondering," said Dad.

Grandpa reached down, took off his prosthetic leg. It was hurting him. He put it on the table. "I like her. She's got her own style."

The Trash King looked at the leg. "Leo, if you ever decide you don't want that leg, I could sell it to a person who has vision."

"You could turn it into a lamp," Mom suggested.

"Or hang it over the fireplace," Dad offered.

Bradley trotted in, took one look at the leg on the table, lowered his tail, and backed out of the room.

Mom and Dad smiled at each other and laughed.

It was a sound Tree hadn't heard from them in the longest time.

He sat on the couch, listening to his parents' laughter.

CHAPTER TWENTY-TWO

Seven A.M. Tuesday morning.

Dad's house. Tree's alarm went off.

This always caused Bradley to at least rise to be let out.

But this morning, Bradley just lay there and looked pleadingly at Tree.

"What's the matter, boy?"

Tree jumped out of bed. "Come on, get up."

Bradley didn't move.

Tree tried to lift him to his feet, but Bradley fell back down.

"Dad!"

Tree knelt by Bradley's side. Bradley's head was down, his breathing forced.

"Dad! . . . It's okay, boy." Tree tried to sound soothing, but the lump of fear in his throat was so big, he could hardly speak.

Dad was in the doorway with shaving cream on his face.

"What's wrong?"

But as soon as he said it, he knew.

Dad bent down by Bradley's old, tired body and put his

hand over Bradley's stomach, which was heaving hard with every breath. He did what Tree had done, tried to get the dog up.

"Aw, Bradley." Dad wiped the shaving cream from his face onto the T-shirt he was wearing. "We've got to call the vet. I think he had some kind of a stroke."

Tree couldn't move.

"I'll call, Tree. You stay with him."

Tree was trying not to cry. He reached in his drawer, got out a dog treat. He stuck it under Bradley's nose. "You want a biscuit?"

Bradley didn't want one.

Dad was back. Hand on Tree's shoulder. "The vet said we need to bring him in. Tree, you understand how old Bradley is."

Tree croaked out, *Can I call Mom?*

"Of course."

"Can she be there? 'Cause she loved him—"

"And he loved her."

Tree carried Bradley to the car, wrapped in a Baltimore Orioles beach towel. Grandpa followed, moving better on his new leg. They drove to Mom's house. She got in the backseat and started to cry.

This helped all the men to be stronger.

They rode to the vet's with Tree saying "Good dog" and Grandpa saying "It's going to be okay, buddy," just like he'd said to so many buddies in the war. Dad forgot the way to the vet's because Mom usually took Bradley, and she had to give him directions, which seemed like old times with a sad new twist.

Dr. Billings brought them right into the examining room. Tree put Bradley gently on the table. Bradley shivered; Tree covered him with the Orioles towel, even though Bradley was more of a Red Sox fan. Dr. Billings looked in Bradley's cloudy eyes, felt around his stomach, listened to his heart. Did what Tree and his father had tried to do, get him to stand.

"He can't," Tree said.

The doctor sighed. "His heart doesn't sound too bad, but I think the rest of him just gave up. He's old. You need to decide what you want to do. I know how hard this is."

Mom put her hand on Bradley's head and wept.

Tree just let loose all the sobs he'd been holding in. Grandpa bent over sadly; Dad lost it, too.

They tried to discuss what to do.

Would they stay when the doctor gave Bradley the shot?

Yes.

Did they want to bury him or have him cremated?

"It doesn't matter," said Dad.

"Buried," said Mom.

Did they understand that the shot would be given and after a few minutes it would go into Bradley's heart and cause it to stop?

Yes, they understood that.

Did they want a few minutes alone first to say good-bye?

Yes. They really did.

■　■　■

Tree didn't know how to say good-bye to a dog he'd known all his life. The sadness of it just washed over him, and because he was big, he had more sadness—at least that's how it seemed. So he stood there with Mom, Dad, and Grandpa and just patted Bradley and said he was a good dog, which is what everyone else was saying. That's when the doctor's cat came into the office. Bradley looked at Tree; their eyes met. And Tree knew Bradley had chased his last cat.

Not even McAllister could save him now.

The doctor came in with his needle, started filling it as the cat walked back and forth, loving the power. Tree wanted to kick the cat out. It wasn't fair to have a cat at Bradley's end. The vet walked over, rubbed Bradley's neck.

Tree stamped his foot at the cat. *"Just go!"* The cat jumped out of the room. Tree looked at Bradley, half dead on the table.

He didn't know he had this many tears inside.

"Well," said the vet, moving closer.

Tree bent over the back half of Bradley, held him tight.

Didn't want him to go through this alone.

"Okay now, Bradley," said the vet. "Okay."

Bradley opened one eye.

Gave half a bark.

Barked for real now.

Shook his head.

Stretched his front paws.

Struggled up like a great old wolf.

Faced the cat, who'd slinked back in.

Tree's mother froze right there.

There are plenty of stories about old dogs who die in their owner's arms, but this isn't one of them.

"Hold on," the vet said, shocked. "Can you put him on the floor, Tree?"

Tree cradled Bradley, lowered him gently down.

"Come on, boy," Grandpa whispered. "Come on."

Bradley walked shakily forward.

The cat scurried into the other room.

Bradley turned slowly, came back.

"I've never seen this happen," the vet said, stunned. "It's your decision, folks. I can't promise how long, but I think this old dog's got some life in him yet."

Tree laughed from sheer relief.

"All right now!" Grandpa shouted.

Dad shook his head, amazed.

Mom couldn't speak.

Bradley looked at Tree, who said, "You want to go home, boy?"

Bradley lay down.

"Home is this way." Tree headed for the door. Bradley got up, walked slowly after him.

The whole town was buzzing with Bradley's near-death experience.

"He probably saw a light going through a tunnel before he turned around," said Mrs. Clitter, who brought over some homemade dog biscuits to celebrate.

She said she'd let McAllister slink by more often to keep Bradley on his toes.

That cat was so irritating, he could keep anything alive.

In the days following Bradley's resurrection, the animals of the neighborhood seemed to come by more to celebrate their friend's return. Tree made sure he always had biscuits in his pocket for any dog who wanted one.

"This is from Bradley," he'd say.

Tree knew it wouldn't last forever, but he decided to focus in full on whatever time was left.

CHAPTER TWENTY-THREE

The basketball season was winding down and Coach Glummer had developed irritable bowel syndrome, which seemed to reach heightened intensity whenever the Pit Bulls were losing by more than twenty points, which was close to always. They were moving down the court in a more unified manner since ballroom dancing; Tree had made some okay handoffs, but it wasn't enough.

Coach Glummer was holding his stomach, shouting that *no one* was paying attention out there. *No one* on this team cared.

Tree stepped forward. "I don't think that's right, Coach. I care. I was paying attention. I know that Petey was trying, and Ryan, and all the guys."

The Pit Bulls, emboldened by this declaration of courage, said yeah, that was right.

Coach Glummer stammered, said they could do better.

"Maybe," said Tree. "But the Huskies were state champs three years in a row. And the last two years they beat us by much bigger point spreads."

The Pit Bulls growled in agreement.

"And we all went to ballroom dancing like you said, and we've been trying to get better."

Tree knew from his grandpa that hard things take time. He decided to not mention this.

Coach Glummer stormed off.

There are two kinds of coaches in the world—those that listen and those that don't. Jeremy Liggins stood back as the Pit Bulls circled Tree, slapped him on the back, and told him, "Way to go, man."

Way to go.

No team had ever told Tree that before.

Helping Grandpa take a shower wasn't easy.

Grandpa was embarrassed he needed help getting in and out of a wet tub, but it was so easy to slip, he needed a spotter, at least for now.

Tree was standing by the tub. Grandpa sat on the plastic stool, using the shower hose to spray the soap off.

That's when they heard the siren.

At first the sound didn't register.

Then a voice on a loudspeaker blared the news:

"This is an evacuation. Move immediately to the Eleanor Roosevelt Middle School. The Burnstown levee broke. Floodwaters are heading toward us."

Tree couldn't believe it. Wasn't there supposed to be more warning than this?

The siren grew louder.

"Okay," said Grandpa. "We move quick and smart."

Tree let Grandpa lean heavily on him to get out of the tub. "Throw me that towel. Get me my leg."

Tree's whole body was shaking. He knew how long it took to get his grandpa dressed.

Dad was working at the store.

It was just them at home. He didn't know how they'd get to the school.

"Get my pants. Get my shirt." Grandpa said it strong, but urgent. "No panic."

Pants on, socks; stump liner; leg clicked into place.

It was going to take forever to walk him down the stairs.

"Call your dad."

Tree raced to the phone. It was dead. Picked up the cell phone. Dialed. No answer.

Dialed again with shaking hands.

Nothing.

"Mom's out of town, Grandpa."

"Call the neighbors. We'll find somebody."

Tree's mind went blank. "I can't remember—"

"Johnsons on the left, Nagels on the right."

Another siren.

"I'm going to call the police, Grandpa. Tell them we need a ride."

He punched 911.

Circuits busy.

CHAPTER TWENTY-FOUR

The front door opened.

"I'm here!" Tree's father shouted.

"We're upstairs, Dad!"

Dad took the stairs three at a time. "We've got to get out fast. Pop, can you move?"

"Slowly. Sorry to be a bother."

"You're no bother. Tree, hold him under the arm." Tree did. Two men trying to carry a third. Too much confusion.

"I've got him, Dad. Grandpa, just hold on."

Tree bent down, slung Grandpa over his shoulder. Felt his muscles sag under the weight.

"I feel like I'm in Vietnam again."

Sirens louder. Dad grabbing food, boots, coats.

"In the car. Come on. We've got to beat it."

Rain lashing outside. Wind railing.

Tree, scared frozen. How could a flood be coming when they hadn't seen it yet?

There wasn't time to go back, to get more clothes, anything

important. Tree thought of his tools and his books and his computer.

In the car Tree remembered Bradley.

"I've got to get Bradley!"

Tree ran back into the house as the sirens grew louder. He found Bradley scared half to death in his room; carried him to the car. Dad trying to drive up the hill. Not easy with the sloshing. Tree looking forward, looking back at the house and wondering what, if anything, would be left. Bradley lay as still as Tree had ever seen him.

The car didn't seem like it could make the hill, started sliding.

Grandpa: "Okay, steady her to the left and crawl it up, that's right, just loose the clutch a bit, ram her forward now."

Inch by inch they slid, slipped, up the muddy hill.

Buses, cars making the trek, packed with scared people. For some reason Tree thought of the photo of his parents laughing. He wished he'd grabbed it. He buried his face in Bradley's fur.

"Good dog," Tree said. "That's a good dog."

It's hard to understand the power of nature when it's unleashed on you like that. Man can walk on the moon, orbit Mars, and cure so many diseases, but no one can stop a raging river once it decides to flood its banks.

At the middle school. A policeman at the door told Tree the impossible.

"No animals in the school, son. I'm sorry. They're being kept at the football field."

"But he'll be scared!"

"They've got some tents. It's the best we can do right now. We've got to get the people inside."

Lightning crashing, rain falling sideways.

Bradley shaking like he's going to explode.

A volunteer fireman asked Tree if he wanted to leave Bradley with him—he'd get him to the shelter.

"No. I'm taking him myself." Tree looked pleadingly at his father, who was helping Grandpa inside.

He gave the fireman Bradley's leash. "Can you hold him just a minute?"

Tree helped Dad get Grandpa into the gym.

They got him settled. Dad took Tree aside. "I don't think I've told you how much help you've been with Grandpa. . . . I don't know what I would have done without you."

"Thanks, Dad. That means a lot."

More people were streaming in.

People shouting if anyone had seen so-and-so as the lightning flashed outside and the thunder sounded like a nightmare. Tree looked up at Eleanor Roosevelt's words carved below the basketball hoop:

No one can make you feel inferior without your consent.

Grandpa was doing his best to help the people around him, like the little girl crying for her mother. Her father kept telling her that Mama was going to be coming through that door any minute, but the little girl kept crying anyway.

"Well, darlin'," said Grandpa. "What color hair does your mother have?"

"Brown." The child sniffed.

"And what's her name, other than Mommy?"

Small voice. "Carol."

"I just happen to know a story about a mother with brown hair named Carol who got stuck in a flood, but she was so smart, she helped a dozen people to safety."

The little girl's eyes were wide.

"You want me to tell you that story?"

"Yes!"

"I've got to take Bradley over to the field, Dad."

"I want you right back."

Tree ran out the door; Bradley was cowering near the fireman's feet.

"Okay, boy, it's okay."

Tree tugged on the leash. Bradley dug his heels in, wouldn't move. Tree bent down to pick him up, saw Mr. Cosgrove walking fast, wearing a big slicker, carrying a flashlight.

That's when Tree got the idea—as clear and clean as taking apart a laser pen.

"Mr. Cosgrove, could we keep some animals in the basement in those storage rooms?"

Mr. Cosgrove stopped, looked at Bradley.

He thought for a moment, then motioned Tree to the back door.

"Thanks." Tree picked up Bradley, carried seventy-four pounds of old, wet dog through the darkened hall.

Mr. Cosgrove unlocked the storage room. "Put those news-papers on the floor and pray we don't get caught."

Tree pictured the vet's office with all those animal cages. If they had cages, they could have more animals in the basement. Tree looked around the big room. It had lots of tall steel file cabinets. He opened some file drawers—they were empty and deep—almost like cages. But he'd need a top so the animals could breathe and not get out.

A loud siren blasted in the distance. Mr. Cosgrove and Tree ran upstairs.

More people were pouring in.

Dad walked over.

"We need to stay together."

Tree told him about Bradley in the basement.

"He'll be all right, Tree, I—"

A little boy let out a huge wail. "But they'll drown! They can't be outside. They can't!"

His father was holding a cage with two white rabbits.

Tree whispered to Mr. Cosgrove, "They've already got a cage."

"Do you know what a pension is?" Mr. Cosgrove snapped.

"Sort of." Tree knew it involved money.

"You know what this could do to my pension?"

The little boy was crying hard.

"*Just* the rabbits and the dog. No more."

Tree carried the rabbits downstairs, told Bradley he had two roommates. Told the rabbits, "This is the greatest guard dog in the universe."

The rabbits looked on, unconvinced, as Bradley slept.

"Tree!" Mr. Cosgrove was holding McAllister, who looked like he'd been drowned nine times. "Some woman said this cat can't stay on the field—it's too sensitive."

McAllister shook, hissed.

Tree: "I can make a cage for him if we have some chicken wire."

"I've got that."

Deep hissing.

Mr. Cosgrove deposited wet, crabby cat in Tree's arms.

Bradley opened one eye.

"No, Bradley."

Bradley rose, barking.

"Bradley, no!"

McAllister arched his back, big meow.

"You guys have to get along."

But certain animal ways are bigger than floods.

Chapter Twenty-five

"What are you doing?" Sully stood at the storage room door.

"Saving animals." Tree put newspaper in a file drawer, lowered McAllister in, covered the top with wire netting, attached it with screws.

"He's not too happy to be saved," Sully observed as McAllister hissed.

"That's the *last* animal." Mr. Cosgrove put the cat in another room.

But more animals were coming.

Tree was running ragged, making cages. He and Sully tried to keep Mr. Cosgrove calm.

"These are just a couple of kittens, Mr. Cosgrove."

"Look what we've got here . . . a ferret."

And the big challenge . . .

"How do you feel about farm animals?"

Three chickens clucked in a cage. "They have arthritis," Sully explained.

News of the flood came sporadically. Radio signals went in and out. Tree was wondering about everything.

Will the house survive?

Will anyone be hurt?

Where in the world is Sophie?

He'd called her house endless times on Dad's cell phone; no answer.

Over and over they heard the warnings: Never stay in your car during a flood. It only takes two feet of water to carry you off.

Amber Melloncroft and Sarah Kravetz shuddered in a corner, blankets over their shoulders.

Tree remembered Grandpa saying how in Vietnam it didn't matter how much money you had, how good you'd been on the football field, how smart you'd been in school.

War is the great equalizer.

Jeremy Liggins stood in the doorway, holding a cage. A policeman told him to bring it outside. Jeremy wailed, "Hamsters can't be in the rain. They're desert animals. *They'll die.*"

Tree walked over. "I might have a safe place for them."

"Where?"

The policeman helped an old woman inside; Tree led Jeremy downstairs.

Mr. Cosgrove stopped when he saw them. *"No."*

"Mr. Cosgrove, Liggins's hamsters will die if they have to be out in the rain."

Mr. Cosgrove took a hard look at Jeremy. He'd heard him say plenty of mean things to Tree.

"You can keep them down here, but *only* because Tree asked. I hope you appreciate a friend like him."

Jeremy looked down, nodded.

"Mr. Cosgrove, you're going to get a medal for being a hero."

"That won't mean much on unemployment."

"This reminds me of Vietnam, Leo." The Trash King huddled under a Red Cross blanket. "Those tropical storms, we'd never get dry. Everything smelled like jungle rot."

"I'll take this over Nam any day."

"Me, too." King's wife, Betty, leaned against his shoulder. "You think there'll be any junk left when we get home, babe?"

"There'll be junk in our lives till we're dead."

Tree watched Grandpa massage his bad leg. King waved an unlit cigar. "A flood like this makes you think. Maybe I should branch out. Get into something current, like hazardous waste."

"You've always been a trendsetter," Betty observed.

Tree's dad came by. "I talked to your Mom in Philadelphia. She's fine. She can't get back yet because of the weather. She sends her love." He smiled. "Her house will probably be okay. It's on a hill. She's worried enough for all of us."

He didn't sound edgy at all when he said it.

Dad's house wasn't on a hill. Tree wondered what that meant.

"I told her how well you've been handling all this, how you're helping out everywhere." Dad grinned. "I told her I was so proud of you, I could bust."

Tree beamed. "Thanks, Dad."

Mayor Diner came in at this point, windblown and wet. She took her slicker off, looked at the horde of people in the gym.

Walked to the free-throw line, smiled sadly.

"Ladies and gentlemen. No one expected to be here tonight."

The people nodded, that's for sure.

"The weather bureau says we could get a lot more rain. That could wipe things out by the river. The sandbags haven't held the way we'd hoped."

Worried looks.

"It's going to be a long night, folks. Whatever you've learned about getting through hard times, I hope you'll share it with the people around you. I've seen so much today that's encouraged me. The bravery of the rescue workers, neighbors helping each other get to safety. It's easy at a time like this to remember all the things we've left behind, but what this town has—the most important part of it—is sitting right here in this place.

"I don't know why these things happen. But I'm asking you to hold on. We'll keep you updated. We'll keep praying. We'll keep looking for it to be over."

Mayor Diner nodded at Inez, the ministry intern at Ripley Presbyterian Church. "Would you lead us in prayer?"

Inez smiled weakly. This flood had her scared stiff. She'd rather have a braver person pray.

But she took the hands of the little girl and the old man next to her; closed her eyes.

"We feel scared, Lord—give us courage. We feel lost—stand beside us. We feel weak—give us strength."

■　■　■

151

Mrs. Clitter had just visited McAllister in the basement. She didn't much like the makeshift cage, but she knew her cat was safe. She had thanked Mr. Cosgrove, gave him some of the homemade fudge that she kept frozen in blocks in her freezer. She'd grabbed pounds of it when the sirens first blared.

You just never know when someone might appreciate something homemade.

A squawk in the hall.

Eli Slovik, completely drenched, was holding a large cage with Fred the parrot inside.

"Back off, Buster," Fred shouted to the policeman who was telling Eli he had to take Fred to the shelter.

"He can't get wet!" Eli screamed.

"There are parrots in the jungle," the policeman shouted. "It gets wet in the jungle!"

Fudge extended, Mrs. Clitter stepped forward.

The officer crumbled, took the bribe.

Mr. Cosgrove ran by; Mrs. Clitter grabbed his arm tight. "Could we ask you to help just one more of God's creatures?"

Eli was praying Fred wouldn't say "Back off, Buster."

"We're full up."

"Not even for this beautiful, rare bird?"

"No more."

Mr. Cosgrove looked at Fred, who looked back and said the words that would save him.

"You're a genius."

Mr. Cosgrove's eyes went soft.

"Now, isn't that something?" Mrs. Clitter marveled.

"You're a genius." Fred made sincere eye contact.

Mr. Cosgrove, struck by the parrot's depth, said, "The bird stays. Make sure he's warm and dry."

"You're a genius," Fred repeated.

"Get him some food. Whatever he wants."

Mr. Cosgrove ran down the stairs, feeling smarter than he had in years.

One man sows, another reaps.

They slept on mats brought by the Red Cross.

They slept in corners wrapped in blankets they had brought from home.

They slept and woke and wondered when it would be over.

Sophie hadn't shown up yet, and Tree was so worried about her, he couldn't sleep.

Cell-phone batteries were out.

Phone lines were down.

Grandpa rigged up a generator so they could watch TV news. The TV cameras captured the mostly flooded town.

"A flood is like a war," Grandpa observed sadly, "because it can take so much with it."

Chapter Twenty-six

The rain stopped Wednesday morning.

The sun, bright and full, announced the new day.

Streets were flooded, cars were overturned.

They'd been in the shelter for two days—living in a time warp.

We just want to get home, the people said.

Home to what?

That was the question.

Grandpa, the Trash King, and Tree were working hard to make sure some of it would be positive.

The sign.

That's the first thing people noticed. It made up for the smell, which was rank and persistent and hung over Ripley like foul gas.

Mildew. Piles of yuck.

It rose from the streets, infiltrated the nostrils.

But the sign.

Grandpa lugged parts of it from his workshop over the

garage; wired it. The Trash King stood on the ladder and balanced it on the roof of Temple Beth Israel—a roof most people could see coming back from the middle school—it overlooked the park, too.

Rabbi Toller turned on the generator.

Tree held the ladder as King fixed the big sign in place.

"Plug her in, Rabbi."

"Let there be light," Rabbi Toller announced.

Pow.

WELCOME HOME, FOLKS
WE'RE GOING TO MAKE IT

People were honking their horns in their trucks, cars, and vans when they saw it.

The Trash King, Tree, and Grandpa grinned as the photographer from the *Ripley Herald* took photo after photo of that sign.

"Why'd you do it?" the reporter asked. "What made you think of it?"

The old soldiers smiled. "We wanted to encourage the town," Grandpa said. "Give people something good to come home to."

They didn't mention the most important part.

You've got to welcome people back when they've been through a war.

Nobody understands that more than a Vietnam vet.

The shock of loss was everywhere.

A flooded-out house is a ghastly sight.

Especially when it's yours.

They'd called the insurance company.

Turned off the electricity.

Tree, Dad, and Grandpa stood on the muck-covered hall carpet wearing white masks passed out by the Public Health Department.

No one spoke.

The couch was soaked and dirty, the stereo was turned upside down, lamps lay broken on the floor, tables upended.

Brown watermarks three feet up on the first-floor walls. Lower kitchen cabinets opened, soaked cereal boxes, broken dishes, piles and piles of what could never be used again.

Tree's clothesline invention hung untouched from the ceiling, casting shadows.

Tree stepped across the mushy rug. He could hardly stand the fumes.

He'd lived in this house most of his life. And now this, too, was going to be a memory.

Grandpa said, "We rebuild with what we've got left."

But there wasn't anything left except the second floor.

The basement windows had popped out.

Five feet of murky water sat in the basement with dirty clothes, empty paint cans, basketballs, and footballs floating on the surface.

Grandpa steadied himself, Old Ironsides.

But Tree wasn't built of such strong stuff.

He couldn't take any more.

He leaned against the dining room wall and started to cry.

Chapter Twenty-seven

"I know what you're thinking," Grandpa said.

Tree sniffed. It's hard to cry when you've got a white mask over your face.

"I bet you're thinking this whole house will have to be torn down."

Tree shrugged. He was, sort of.

"I can see why you'd think that, having never built a house before." Grandpa studied the wall. "See, floods leave clues. We can see how high the water went on the first floor. Everything above the waterline is okay. The mirrors, the hanging lights. We've got a whole second floor in mint condition. Now, inside the wall . . ." He put an arm on Tree's shoulder to steady himself and kicked a hole in the wall with his good foot. He stuck his hand in, pushed past insulation. "We can see that the plumbing pipes still look solid. I'll have to rewire where it got wet, but we haven't lost the farm. Not by a long shot."

"We haven't?"

Grandpa handed Tree a hammer. "Ram that there."

Tree hit the wall, made a hole.

"Rip it out."

Tree did.

"Stick your hand in there until you feel the frame."

Tree pushed through the insulation. "I can feel it."

"Knock on it."

Tree rapped strong. It was solid.

"We're going to lug this mess out of here, strip this Sheetrock down to the frame, and build her back up again."

Tree sighed. "You make it sound so easy, Grandpa."

"It's not going to be easy. It's going to be worth it."

They stayed in a hotel that night. Bradley, too.

Tree was so tired and sore from cleaning up.

Dad called Curtis and Larry at school. Both wanted to come home in a few days to help.

They sure could use the extra hands.

Then Tree called Sophie's house and finally got an answer.

He almost shouted for joy when he heard her voice.

"I tried to call you, Tree, for the last three days, but I couldn't get through. Aunt Peach got us a room at a motel. We were all shoved in there with cots and cats. It was torture. But the apartment's fine. The flood didn't touch us. I guess there's something good about a fourth-floor walk-up."

He told her about Dad's house and how hard they were working.

"I'm sorry you lost out. But it's good you're not average

size, Tree. It's good your dad and grandpa have a really big guy to help take care of business."

Tree squared his shoulders at that one.

Two of Grandpa's friends brought an electric pump to drain water from the basement.

Dad and Tree picked through the kitchen and garage, finding what could be saved.

They worked like machines while they still had daylight, wearing big rubber gloves. Floodwater is infectious.

Lugged trash to the Dumpster in the driveway.

Every house on Tree's street had one.

Tree shoveled out piles of junk from the first floor into the Dumpster, smiling bravely at other neighbors who were doing the same thing.

Tree worked till he couldn't anymore. Then the momentousness took over.

There was too much to do. How could they *ever*—

"The first rule of rebuilding is to find something positive and concentrate on that," Grandpa said.

Tree looked at the flooded, smelly mess. "I haven't thrown up yet."

Grandpa laughed. "That's a start."

The basement water had been drained, leaving rank, thick sediment that covered the floor and walls.

Sophie threw ruined books and sports equipment into garbage bags. She'd come to help Tree with the cleanup.

Tree looked at the broken trophy case lying open on the muddy basement floor—Curtis's and Larry's sports certificates were all ruined. Some of the trophies were cracked.

They'd seemed so important when he was growing up.

Tree knelt down to touch a frame with smashed glass. He remembered his mother framing Curtis's award for basketball. Remembered being in the high school auditorium when Curtis got it. Tree had applauded so hard, his hands hurt.

Tree picked up Larry's brass home run medal and Curtis's athlete of the year trophy, dripping mud.

All that glory covered in sludge.

Tree put them in a box.

"I'm going outside before I puke," Sophie announced, lugging a bag up the stairs.

The Trash King picked through the rubble of what was left in his junkyard—so much of it had been ruined by the flood.

"You look at this red wagon," he said to Tree, who'd come to help him move some of the heavy pieces. "Why did it survive? It should have been sucked up by the wind—carried down the river. But it's here. That tells me it can take the heat. I'm not going to sell it for peanuts. I want some real cash for a tough piece like this."

He walked over piles of rusted metal, lifted an old weather vane from the heap. Stuck it in the ground; the vane pointed north. "Still working," he declared, "after all we've been through. You can look at this yard of mine, think there's nothing left worth saving. But trash is here to remind us all that the old's not so bad—it's got life in it yet."

He looked toward the sun, scratched his chin. "I'm going to put that in the brochure."

The giant oak tree began to bud five days after the flood.

Birds were chirping in its branches.

Not one limb was out of place.

Benches were upended, lesser trees snapped in two.

It makes you appreciate a serious root system; roots planted so deep in the ground, holding steady against the storm.

Tree stood in front of the tree with Sophie. Every day at Dad's they were making progress. A huge dehumidifier was in the basement now, drying things up. They'd ripped up the carpet, lugged it out to the street.

"I know this is a special park for you, Tree. I like nature, but too much of it makes me nervous." A tear rolled down Sophie's cheek.

Tree bent down. "What's wrong?"

"I didn't tell you 'cause you had so much going on, but Lassie . . . she didn't make it."

"Oh, no."

"It happened at the motel. She was crawling so slow. Then she just froze on the branch. I tried to get her to do the dance, but she couldn't do it anymore." Big sniff. "I told her, 'I know what it's like to not have anyone like you around. You feel like giving up sometimes.'"

Tree took her hand.

"I told her that, as a pet, she'd been true. She didn't fetch or do tricks, but she gave back as much as a reptile can. She fell off the branch, hit the floor of the cage." Sophie lowered her head. "I buried her in the Dumpster in the parking lot. I said, 'Thanks, girl, for everything. You could have been a dog if you'd had better luck.'"

"You were good to her," Tree said. "You gave her a good life."

Sophie nodded. "God knows I tried."

Tree looked across the park to the roof of Temple Beth Israel, where the sign was still welcoming people home.

Just then, Nuts the squirrel showed up, nervous as anything.

"Hey, Nuts. You made it." Tree threw him a peanut; the squirrel grabbed it, studied Sophie.

"You know this squirrel?"

"Kind of." Tree felt stupid.

"He looks like he's got a lot to deal with."

Nuts shook a little, scampered off.

"So are you sleeping in the park or what, with your dad's house all messed up?"

Tree grinned. "Actually, my mom's house made it through fine. She invited us to stay with her until Dad's house gets fixed."

Sophie snorted. "Your dad, too?"

"Even Bradley. She said it was going to take a lot of work to get the house right, that no one should have to sleep in a hotel, and that she and Dad were adults and could handle this. We're going there tonight."

Sophie looked at the white oak. "You've got a strange family, Tree."

Tree didn't say it, but he thought this was a very good sign. Maybe his mother wanted to work things out with his father.

He wondered if something awful, like a flood, could have a good side.

CHAPTER TWENTY-EIGHT

Dad, Tree, Grandpa, and Bradley stood on Mom's front porch.

They had been working hard at the house. They looked and smelled it, too.

Dad rang the bell. "Okay," he said nervously. "This is going to be fine."

Tree bit his lip, hoping like crazy.

Mom answered the door, looking really pretty in a blue sweater and skirt.

Her hands went up. "You're *early.*"

Bradley went right to her.

Dad croaked, "You said come before dinner."

"I *said* come *after* dinner."

"We can come back," said Dad.

"No, just come in. Tree, wipe your feet. Leo, how are you?" They came inside. "This is going to be a little complicated, but we're all adults."

I'm twelve, Tree thought. *I just look older.*

The doorbell rang.

Mom smoothed her skirt, announced shrilly, "I have a date."

Her first date in twenty-three years.

"Oh," Dad said strangely.

Doorbell again.

"And that's him. So we're all just going to deal with it."

She smiled too bright, opened the door to Richard Blunt, an average-size, average-looking person.

"Richard," Mom said.

"Jan, you look lovely."

Grandpa sniffed.

Tree coughed.

Dad shoved his hands into his pockets.

Conan spoke for them all—hurled himself in complete fury at Richard Blunt's ankle with a clear purpose: tearing it to shreds.

"Bad dog!" Mom grabbed Conan, handed him to Tree.

Good dog, Tree thought as Conan flailed.

"Are you all right?" Mom asked. "He's never done that before."

Richard Blunt nodded warily.

"Richard, this is my son Tree."

Hand extended. "You're back from college?"

Tree shook it. "I'm in middle school."

Richard Blunt looked up.

"And due to the flood, I have some houseguests." Mom glared at Dad, who was dank and damp and looked like he'd slept in the park. "Richard, this is my ex . . . this is my former . . . *this is the father of my children.*"

"How's it going?" Dad said.

Richard Blunt nodded.

"And *this*," Mom said, "is my former father . . . I mean . . . in-law . . ."

Grandpa took a lurching step forward, shook hands.

Not to be forgotten, Bradley walked to Mom's side.

"And *this*," Mom shouted, *"is my former dog."*

Bradley's cloudy eyes looked up in undying loyalty.

There is no such thing as a former dog.

It was a toss-up as to which was worse.

The introductions, or when Mom and Richard Blunt tried to leave.

The front door was stuck. And Tree, trying to help, made the mistake of putting Conan down, which caused Conan to go back to his original idea of tearing Richard Blunt's ankle to bloody shreds, which caused Mom to shriek, *"Remove that animal!"* as she raced out the door.

Tree, Dad, and Grandpa stood there. No one knew what to say.

Then, finally . . .

Dad: "That guy's a real turkey."

Grandpa: "He has sneaky eyes. I don't trust him."

Tree didn't say what he was thinking.

He couldn't believe his mother would go out with anyone except his father.

He couldn't believe he'd thought that all this togetherness was a good idea.

They cooked pasta in the kitchen and ate it silently.

They waited at the kitchen table until she came home.

She walked into the kitchen, saw the dirty dishes.

"You could have at least cleaned up," she snarled at Dad, who said nothing, which never helped.

Then Dad unfolded the new sleep-away couch too hard and busted the spring, and it sat there, half opened—a huge, broken thing. He lugged the mattress onto the floor.

"I'll leave in the morning, Jan. Get a hotel room."

"Oh, yes," she shouted, "make *me* the unreasonable one."

"You don't need any help with that," he muttered.

Tree was listening from the kitchen, doing the dishes. Grandpa had gone to bed. Don't fight, he thought.

Too late.

"How *typical*," she shouted, "to use sarcasm."

Dad said sarcasm was better than hair-trigger emotion.

"You always need the last word, don't you, Mark?"

"Whatever you say, Jan."

Tree wanted to march in there, tell them they were both wrong.

Stop fighting. He wanted to shout it.

Just for tonight, can't you stop fighting?

Slam. That was her bedroom door.

Dad got the last word.

But Mom got the last sound.

CHAPTER TWENTY-NINE

Curtis and Larry showed up the next day and bunked in sleeping bags at Mom's.

Dad was at a motel.

Grandpa stayed at Mom's, too, with Tree and Bradley, but this afternoon he was out with the Trash King getting building supplies.

"How bad is it?" Curtis asked Tree.

Part of Tree wanted to say, "It's awful with Mom and Dad," but he knew Curtis didn't mean that.

Tree tried to find the words, but you've got to see for yourself what a flood can do.

Curtis and Larry walked around the muddy lawn, kicked debris away, looked in the broken basement windows.

They went inside the house, came out gagging.

Larry swore, hit the Dumpster, stormed off to get away from the sight.

Curtis went after him. Motioned Tree over. Put one arm

around Larry, one around Tree, and they stood there looking at the old house.

Tree felt so close to his brothers.

"We've got seventy-two hours," Curtis said. "What do we do first?"

"Give up," Larry suggested.

Curtis shook his head, held on tight.

"Scrub the basement walls and floor with Clorox," Grandpa ordered. "No joke."

Rubber gloves on, face masks tight, the Benton brothers formed a fighting unit to kill all bacteria left by the dirty floodwaters.

They lugged ruined boxes of photos and videos to the street.

Grandpa demonstrated how you pull down Sheetrock walls.

Slammed a sledgehammer into the wall, yanked as much out as he could with a crowbar.

Tree and his brothers stood by the wall, holding sledgehammers, too. No one wanted to go first.

Finally, Curtis said, "I keep thinking how it used to be, how Mom drove us crazy picking out the paint for the walls. It's stupid. I don't want to knock them down."

Larry dropped his hammer. "I don't, either."

Tree wanted a magical wind to dry everything up and put it back in place.

"You've got to take a thing apart before you can fix it," Grandpa explained.

Tree, Curtis, and Larry looked at one another.

"The best thing about a sledgehammer is how it lets you release your frustrations." Grandpa pounded his into the wall. "You fellas should try it."

Three sledges rammed the wall.

Grandpa shouted, *"And watch the plumbing in there!"*

Larry went at this with everything he had.

A clang and a crack.

Larry hit a pipe.

Grandpa limped over, marked the crack with tape. "You got many more frustrations left?"

Larry gulped. "Not too many."

"Good. Watch how your brother does it." Grandpa motioned to Tree. "He hits it just right. Swings easy, keeps up a steady rhythm."

Tree liked hearing that, but he wasn't sure Larry would. He hit the wall with the sledge to demonstrate, ripped off the wallboard. Hit it again.

Larry tried, but wasn't getting it.

"Here." Tree stood behind him, held his arm back, let it go. "Hit it like this."

Larry tried it himself.

"That's it," Tree said.

By night, they'd knocked the wallboard down in the hall and the living room.

They pulled out the insulation.

Those rooms stood stark like a tree without leaves.

Dad came in, beat—he had to work at the store *and* help at the house.

Stared at the sight. "You guys did all this?"

"I did most of it," Larry said.

Tree and Curtis pounced on him.

Two A.M.

Tree was in his room at Mom's house. It felt good to be clean, felt good to be someplace that didn't smell like sewage.

He'd scrubbed Larry's home run medal and Curtis's athlete of the year trophy in hot, soapy water.

Dried them off.

Poured metal polish on a cloth and began to rub the medal. He went over and over it, let it dry. Did the same thing with Curtis's brass cup.

He rubbed the dried polish off. Still a few scratches, but the metal looked gold again.

Took another cloth, polished both pieces till they shone.

He sprayed Windex on the marble base of Curtis's trophy to make it gleam.

The trophy looked good, but Curtis's name in raised black letters wasn't clear. He filled in the C, the T, the BENTON with a laundry marker.

Turned to the medal. It was in an open leather box. The box had water stains all over. It looked awful. Tree had seen his dad restore a baseball glove left in the rain with saddle soap.

He poured saddle soap onto a damp cloth and cleaned the box.

That made it better, but not good enough.

He opened a can of mink oil—put some on a cloth, rubbed it deep into the grain.

You've got to be patient to fix a thing right.

He felt the leather get softer, rubbed more and more mink oil in. Gradually, the color deepened. The water stains disappeared.

Tree rubbed for an hour until he'd restored it to something you'd be proud to put on a shelf.

He fell into bed at 4:30.

CHAPTER THIRTY

"It's going to be better here now." Curtis surveyed the first floor of Dad's house. They'd gotten all the wallboard off, down to the frame and joints.

A contractor friend of Grandpa's was going to put up new walls next week.

Curtis and Larry were heading back to school.

"One game!" Larry ran outside, got the basketball that survived the flood.

Curtis ran outside as Larry dribbled the ball in the driveway. They'd hosed the driveway down. It was clean now.

"Come on," Larry shouted. Passed the ball to Tree.

Tree bounced, passed to Curtis, who made an easy basket. Larry got the ball under the net. Passed it to Tree again.

"Come on."

Larry got in front of Tree to guard him; all arms.

Tree tried to get around him.

Larry laughed.

Tree tried a basket from too far away.

Missed.

Curtis threw the ball back to him. Larry got out of the way.

"Nice and easy," Curtis said. "Set up the shot, then shoot."

Tree did that. Watched in triumph as the ball popped through the net.

"Awesome, Tree Man," Curtis said.

Larry slapped him on the back.

It was one of those moments you want to cover with plastic to keep safe.

Dad pulled up in the car with Grandpa, honked the horn.

"We've got to go," Curtis said.

"Wait. I have something for you guys." Tree ran to the porch, grabbed the presents wrapped in tissue paper. Handed one to Larry, one to Curtis.

"Open them."

Dad and Grandpa were heading up the walk.

Larry tore his open.

Couldn't believe what he saw.

Curtis unwrapped his carefully, held it solemnly to the light.

"I washed them off and gave them a polish. That's all it took," Tree said.

Larry touched the leather box, ran his finger across his name. "I thought it was gone." He looked up at Tree.

Tree shrugged.

Dad stepped forward to say something, but Grandpa motioned him back.

Larry slapped Tree on the shoulder. The slap turned into a hug.

Curtis put an arm around Tree, an arm around Larry.

"We'll be back on Memorial Day," Curtis promised.

"Try to get the house finished by then," Larry added. "And don't grow anymore, okay?"

Over the next weeks, Tree knew something had changed.

In school, he and Sophie walked down the hall and Amber and her friends moved aside fast when they saw them coming.

At Dad's, Grandpa started rewiring the downstairs. The new walls went up, and what had seemed like a construction site began to feel like a home again.

At Mom's, Tree looked at the picture of his parents laughing at the beach, and for the first time, he didn't get too torn up about it.

Mom sat him down. "How are you doing with the divorce stuff? How are you feeling about it?"

Tree said honestly, "I wish you hadn't done it. I wish you and Dad had tried harder to stay together. But I'm okay, Mom. I'm okay."

Phantom pain does get better.

CHAPTER THIRTY-ONE

Rat a tat tat tat.

Rat a tat tat.

Luger hit the snare drum two-handed.

Rrrrrrrrrrrrrrrrrrrrrrrrrrrrrrrrrrrrrrrrrrrrrrrrrrrrrrrrrr.

Drumsticks rolled.

"Move it out!" the Trash King shouted.

The Vietnam vets marched in formation as the Ripley Memorial Day Parade began.

The vets were right behind the League of Women Voters float honoring the women's suffrage movement. Mayor Diner, as Susan B. Anthony, was chained to a post, screaming that women need the right to vote.

Rat a tat tat.

Grandpa was marching next to the Trash King, swinging his right leg out as sharp and smooth as he could manage.

People lined the streets four deep, applauding, whistling.

No town needed a parade as badly as Ripley.

And now, Scotty McInerny, decorated twice for courage in

battle, nodded to Luger, lifted his bagpipes to his mouth, and let the first mournful wail of "The Highlander's March" rise from that instrument.

A bagpipe and a snare drum make everybody stand a little taller.

Tree held the American flag and marched alongside Grandpa.

He was there in case Grandpa pushed too hard. If he did, he'd be riding in the Army Jeep driven by Wild Man Finzolli, who was honking the horn and waving to the crowd like he was running for governor. Bradley was sitting in the passenger seat.

Tree raised the flag high. It caught the wind, billowed full.

He felt so proud.

Raising a flag is the best thing going.

Rat a tat tat.

Rat a tat tat tat.

Rrrrrrrrrrrrrrrrrrrrrrrrrrrrrrrrrrrrrrrrrrrrrrrrrrrrrrrrrrrrrrrrrrrrrr.

They marched.

Not for themselves.

They marched to remember the ones who didn't make it back.

They marched because seeing so much loss can teach you about life.

They marched because we're all fighting a war whether we know it or not—a war for our minds and souls and what we believe in.

Bagpipe sounds rising in the air, overcoming the Eleanor Roosevelt Middle School marching band a block ahead, struggling through the only known band rendition of "(I Can't Get No) Satisfaction."

Vets from World War II, Korea, the Gulf War.

Kids on Rollerblades.

Realtors in flag shirts.

Riding lawn mowers driven by Ace Hardware employees.

The high school jazz band blowing strong.

Grandpa feeling wobbly, but he didn't want to stop.

Luger was behind him, watching.

The drummer is always in charge.

Luger slowed the beat.

Grandpa marched slower; his limp was getting worse.

"Grandpa, are you okay?"

Pushing, frustrated. But he was too stubborn to stop.

Tree moved closer. "Grandpa, I'm worried you're going to hurt yourself."

Mona Arnold was standing by the halfway mark at the parade route with her husband and son.

She watched the Vietnam vets marching sharp, except for Leo.

He looked at her, looked away.

He tried to walk better, but his leg was hurting.

She was alongside him now.

"Enough of this, Leo. I want you to ride."

"A half mile more," he said. Keep pushing. Just like Vietnam.

"This isn't about making it until the end or you lose. You already went farther than I figured you could."

"You losing faith in me, Mona?"

"I'm losing patience."

The Trash King and the vets stopped marching.

Tree held the flag high.

Bradley barked.

"We're all just ordinary heroes here, Leo," the Trash King said. "No supermen allowed. Get in the Jeep."

"All right, all right." Grandpa climbed in good leg first, yanked up the other. Bradley crawled in the back.

Wild Man sounded the horn. "You did real good, Leo."

Grandpa took off his fake leg and raised it over his head.

Wild applause from the crowd.

Sophie, dressed like a soldier of yesteryear, was standing with Tree by the big white oak. They were waiting for Mayor Diner to change out of her Susan B. Anthony costume so the rest of the Memorial Day festivities could begin.

"I stand here in this park, Tree, and I see your story."

"What do you mean?"

"Look at these plants. There's a bush that isn't exciting. There's a vine that means nothing. There's a bunch of weeds. And there's this tree that you can't ignore." She hit the bark. "It sticks out like a sore thumb. That's who you are."

Tree liked that thought, except for the sore-thumb comparison.

Mayor Diner was onstage now.

"Aunt Peach wants me to march in place while I'm playing my solo and salute when I'm done."

Tree wasn't sure about that. "Be yourself, you know?"

179

Sophie cleared her throat and spat big into a tissue.

They walked to the stage.

She played her flute medley of great war hits with true feeling for the instrument, even though the wind blew her cap of yesteryear off during "Yankee Doodle." Tree could tell she was getting a mouthful of spit toward the end of "Over There," but he bet he was the only one to notice. She got a great round of applause from everyone except the popular eighth-grade girls, but the unpopular seventh-grade boys and Aunt Peach more than made up for it.

Mrs. Clitter and the Senior Women's Modern Dance Society formed the Memorial Day teardrop that symbolized the loss and courage of those who had died to make this country free.

Mayor Diner read, "In Flanders fields the poppies blow / Between the crosses, row on row . . ."

Then Inez, the ministry intern from Ripley Presbyterian Church, walked forward carrying a large candle, followed by the town's clergy.

She faced the crowd as a strong wind blew, and said the words she'd been practicing over and over.

"We light this candle of hope to help us remember that hope can always be with us. We light this candle to thank God for helping us through the flood. We light this candle of hope now . . ."

She struck a large match, but the wind blew it out.

Tried again.

"We light this candle of hope now . . ."

A flicker on the candle this time, but the wind was too strong.

A few ministers surrounded her.

"We light this candle of hope . . ."

"Lord," shouted Rabbi Toller. "We need a blowtorch."

"We light this candle of hope . . ."

Not today, they didn't.

Inez turned to the crowd, her big moment snuffed out. She was going to have to write this up for her weekly intern report.

"It's a metaphor, okay? We'll just be hopeful—no flame."

"Amen," said the people.

Sophie pushed Tree forward.

"What?"

"You're bigger than those people. Stand in front of the candle. Stop the wind. You can do it!"

No. Tree couldn't.

"Go on!" She shoved him forward.

Sully walked up, slapped him on the back. "That wind is history."

Inez gazed up as Tree, embarrassed, lumbered across the stage. "I can stop the wind, maybe."

He smiled. Not many kids could say that.

Tree stood over the candle, tucked in, felt the wind trying to crash past him.

Inez shouted, "We light this candle of hope to remember that hope can always be with us. . . ." She looked at Tree.

"Light it!" he said.

She lit it.

The flame caught, burned.

Tree guarded the flame until it got serious.

Inez raised the candle, triumphant.

The people applauded.

"I told you!" Sophie screamed from the crowd.

"Yes!" Sully stamped his feet. "Yes!"

Tree felt like he'd just made a winning free throw in the fourth quarter.

Cameras flashed, flags waved.

His mom smiled proudly from one end of the crowd.

His dad smiled proudly from the other.

Curtis and Larry were clapping and shouting.

Tree looked at his grandpa, and he could see the face of war and peace right there, backlit by the sun.

McInerny lifted his bagpipes and played "From the Halls of Montezuma," which was the Marines' song. McInerny himself was in the Army, but he thought the Marines had a better tune.

The purpose of a bagpipe is to reach deep into the heart.

Everything's got a purpose, really—you just have to look for it.

Cats are good at keeping old dogs alive.

Loss helps you reach for gain.

Death helps you celebrate life.

War helps you work for peace.

A flood makes you glad you're still standing.

And a tall boy can stop the wind so a candle of hope can burn bright.